SECRET NINJA SPIES

CHAMPION TAKEDOWN

ALEX KO

With special thanks to Rosie Best

First published in the UK in 2012 by Usborne Publishing Ltd., Usborne House, 83-85 Saffron Hill, London EC1N 8RT, England. www.usborne.com

Series created by Working Partners Limited.
Text copyright © Working Partners Limited, 2012
Illustrations copyright © Usborne Publishing Ltd., 2012
Illustrations by Kanako and Yuzuru.

The name Usborne and the devices ♀ ⊕ are Trade Marks of Usborne Publishing Ltd.

A CIP catalogue record for this book is available from the British Library.

ISBN 9781409522041 JFMA JJASOND/12 00500/1
Printed in Reading, Berkshire, UK.

Chapter One

Josh Murata spun through the air like a cyclone, twisting to meet the flying target as it came towards him. His right foot struck out with a force that could have knocked one of Yoshida Noboru's gangster henchmen out stone cold. His shoe hit its target with a *thunk*…and the ball soared through the air, past the goalkeeper's outstretched hands, into the makeshift goal and out the other side.

"Sorry!" Josh held up his hands to the other kids

who'd gathered to play football in the park. "I'll get it."

As he jogged after the ball, a cheer rose up. A crowd of people stretched all along one side of the park, lining the road. Some of them were waving banners. Several kids at the skatepark next to the road had climbed up on top of the ramp for a better look.

Josh just caught sight of his bright red and yellow ball as it rolled between the legs of the crowd. *I can't lose it,* he thought. *I've already destroyed three balls!* He dived after it.

"Sorry!" he called, as he pushed through the forest of legs, dodging one lady's dangling handbag and nearly braining himself on the flagpole of a drooping Japanese flag. "Sorry! 'Scuse me! *Sumimasen...*"

The ball skidded away from his fingertips. It rolled underneath a plastic barrier and across the road, under the thundering feet of a herd of running men and women. Josh straightened up. There were runners as far as he could see. Some were dressed in professional-looking Lycra and shiny running shoes, but most looked like amateurs, in T-shirts and jogging trousers. There were even a few people wearing fancy dress, including a four-person dragon and one man in an enormous Godzilla costume.

"Josh?" he heard Jessica call out from somewhere behind him.

"Over here!"

Jessica *sumimasen*ed her way through the crowd to his side and leaned over the barrier.

"I lost Naoko's ball," said Josh, gesturing to the other side of the road where the ball had rolled, through the feet of the runners and into a crowd even larger than the one on their side.

"Well, there goes the last of this week's pocket money," Jessica said. But she was smiling, watching Godzilla stomping along surrounded by sweating athletes with looks of painful concentration on their faces. "I didn't know there was a race today," she said.

"I thought there weren't as many runners in the park as usual," Josh mused. "They're all here, instead of doing laps around the temple and the lake."

"It's a fun run. Look, there are the organizers." Jessica pointed down the street to a table draped in a banner saying, *Tokyo Fun Run, raising money for the new Tokyo Sports Academy*. The table was laden with hundreds of little bottles of water. A runner snatched one up as he dashed past.

"They hardly need to promote running – I mean, Tokyo is already running mad." Josh had to raise his voice to be heard over a swell of cheering that seemed to roll down the street towards them. "You can't walk from Granny's building to the skatepark without feeling like you're in a marathon..."

The noise kept on rising, louder and louder, until the people on all sides of Josh were screaming and chanting.

"Mizuki! Mizuki!"

Josh caught his breath.

"*Banzai*, *okaasan*, the Marathon Princess!" yelled a little girl just to Josh's left, tugging on her mother's sleeve and pointing.

"*Ganbatte*, Mizuki!" yelled her mother. "You can do it!"

Josh grinned as his glance followed the little girl's pointing finger to a slender young woman in purple running gear with a cropped pixie-style haircut. He'd read an article about her just that morning – even

English-language manga magazines wanted to get close to the best marathon runner Japan had ever known.

"You're the greatest, Mizuki!" Josh shouted, as the Marathon Princess came closer, but he couldn't hear his own voice over the screaming all around him.

Jessica nudged him, grinned widely and mouthed the word, "*Legend!*"

Josh had to agree. Mizuki had always been popular as a runner, but ever since her performance in last year's New York Marathon, she'd become legendary. The media had been full of her story – how she'd got cramp in the first five miles, only to give herself an impromptu shiatsu massage with cameras popping all around her. She'd come back not only to complete the marathon but to win it! Now, shiatsu therapists throughout Tokyo were claiming to have taught her and she was known for being the bravest and luckiest athlete to come out of Japan. Some people even said that touching Mizuki would give you good luck for a year! Josh turned back, not wanting to miss a second of her incredible stride, full of grace and power...

But there was something wrong. Why was she this

far back? And as she came closer, Josh saw that she didn't have her usual laser-like focus on the way ahead. Her eyes kept flicking from one side of the road to the other, as if she was scanning the crowd.

Suddenly an arm stretched out across the barriers, reaching for Mizuki. The Marathon Princess yelped and took a leap sideways, losing control of her stride. She veered towards the crowd on the other side of the road. Hands reached out there too, and someone's outstretched fingers brushed Mizuki's shoulder.

There was a scream, so loud Josh heard it even above the roar of the crowd. "I touched her!"

As if on cue, the crowd around Josh pushed forwards, pressing him up against the barrier with a force that made his ribs ache. He tried to push back, but the plastic started to buckle. Beside him, Jessica was shouting something, but he couldn't hear – and then the next barrier along snapped and people started pouring through. Josh saw the little girl's mother trying to shelter her as people shoved to get past.

Josh's heart beat like a pneumatic drill – the fans were heading for Mizuki. But she was a runner after all, she'd outpace them, right?

Mizuki stumbled. She was going much more slowly now, and as she finally drew level with Josh and Jessica, he could see she was unnaturally pale. It wasn't just the stampede – Mizuki didn't look well.

"If she faints, she'll be crushed by her own fans!" Jessica yelled into his ear. "We have to do something!"

Josh threw himself forward, somersaulting over the barrier, and Jessica followed. They rolled clear just as the barrier broke, spilling more stumbling fans onto the road. Josh got to his feet and sprang forwards just in time to draw level with Mizuki. "We want to help!" he shouted. "Er...*tetsudaimasu!*"

"Help...?" Mizuki gasped, turning her head towards him. There was a dazed look in her eyes.

"Trust us!" shouted Jessica, popping up on the other side of Mizuki.

Josh held out his hand. For a second the three of them ran on side by side, and then Mizuki reached out and put her hand into his.

Jessica nodded up ahead to the gap in the crowd where the Fun Run organizers stood behind their table full of water bottles, blocking the entrance to a small side street. "Follow me!"

They raced up to the table and Jessica took an abrupt turn to the left, her trainers skidding on the road, dodging around the table. Mizuki and Josh followed. The organizers watched them, open-mouthed, and Josh couldn't resist giving them a cheeky wave.

The side street was empty, but Josh looked back and saw hundreds of people still running after them, reaching out for Mizuki. He twisted his leg in a back kick and caught the edge of the table, tipping it up and sending bottles of water spilling across the street as the organizers leaped back. Josh breathed a sigh of relief as the pursuers tripped up on the rolling bottles. The makeshift barricade had worked! But Mizuki was slowing down again. He could hear her breathing rasping in her chest like she was a zombie. Drops of sweat clung to her eyelashes and the spiky ends of her hair, spraying off with every heavy footfall as she jogged along.

"*Arigatō*," she whispered. "Thank you, very..." She stumbled and Josh and Jessica lunged forward, each taking one of her arms. Mizuki let them support her on their shoulders and they jogged down the side street together.

"We have to get you away from here," Josh muttered. "Our granny's apartment is close, you can go there and rest."

Mizuki nodded.

"We can't take the main roads," Jessica pointed out, over Mizuki's drooping head. "There'll be another stampede."

"I can get us there through the backstreets, I think," Josh said. He remembered the time he'd helped Nana Sato, Team O's surveillance expert, to give Mr. Nakamura directions as he chased down a jewel thief carrying a bugged diamond necklace.

Just an ordinary Tuesday afternoon at Sakura Apartments... Josh smiled at the thought. When he and Jess had come to Japan to stay with their Granny Murata they'd had no idea that she was the leader of Team Obaasan, a group of crack crime-fighters who were all geriatrics. The Sakura Apartments where she lived turned out to be no ordinary retirement home, but the secret base for these elderly ninja spies!

"Turn right here," he said, and the three of them went down an alley between two buildings. They hobbled past a row of parked cars and bins full of packaging. Sweet cooking smells spilled out into the alley. Josh frowned in concentration. They needed to keep going diagonally, and when they hit the main shopping street they'd have to take a detour behind the bicycle shop…

He almost tripped over his feet as Jessica and Mizuki skidded to a halt.

"Josh!" Jessica hissed. "What now?"

The street ahead was packed with people carrying baskets and peering at a row of busy stalls. Hundreds of blue and yellow coloured flags were draped over the stalls and out of the windows of the buildings. It was a fish market!

"Can't go back. Come on, before they see us," Josh said, and he steered Mizuki quickly through a small gap behind the stalls. They came to a barricade of plastic boxes, and had to squeeze past, holding their breath. Josh went through last, and he was just breathing out with relief that they'd all made it when he felt his right foot skid out from under him, the world dropping away with a sickening lurch. He braced himself against the wall as the piece of ice slithered across the road.

"Careful!" Jessica gasped. "I don't think you want to fall in *that*."

Josh sucked in a deep breath and looked down to see a barrel full of live, wriggling squid with gooey eyes and tentacles reaching out for him.

"Let's get out of here," Josh said, placing his feet carefully between the scattered pieces of ice.

They turned a corner and dashed across an intersection. Mizuki was slowing down again, but she managed to keep going as they passed a dancing Stormtrooper...

Josh twisted his neck in a double take, but he hadn't hallucinated – it really was the dancing Stormtrooper, a man in a black and white sci-fi uniform who danced on Tokyo street corners. Josh grinned. If anyone was filming him while Mizuki and the twins staggered past, that clip would go viral on the internet for a whole different reason...

"Mizuki!" a shrill voice rang out.

Oh no. Josh risked a glance over his shoulder, and

cringed as he saw a schoolgirl in a straw hat pointing out Mizuki to her friends – all twenty of them. A chorus of high-pitched squeals and shrieking broke out. Josh turned back and put his head down, trying to ignore the piercing cries.

"I want to run with Mizuki!"

"Marathon Princess, be my good-luck charm!"

"It's okay," he said, although he could hear the pounding of forty hard-heeled school shoes on the road behind them. "Keep going! We're nearly—"

They skidded around a corner, and Josh's heart swelled and then sank into his boots. In front of them was the little kabuki theatre just one block away from Granny's apartment…and in front of the theatre there was a crowd of people, just coming out after a performance. They all turned, stared at Mizuki and the twins in astonishment for a second, and then started to move towards them.

"Trapped!" Jessica gasped. Josh cast a glance back along the road. The swarm of schoolgirls was catching up with them.

Beside him, Mizuki finally stopped putting one foot in front of the other, and sagged.

"Don't faint," Josh muttered, though Mizuki's eyes were drooping shut and her weight on his arm was growing heavier. "Please don't faint..." He grappled round to put an arm around her waist, holding her body as she slumped further against him.

The theatre crowd was nearly on them now. Some of them had broken into a run and others were fishing in their bags for pens and notebooks.

Does she look like she can sign an autograph right now? Josh drew himself up, ready to defend Mizuki from her adoring fans.

"Josh-kun, let go!"

Josh looked down. A familiar pair of sharp grey eyes peered up at him through the slit in a black mask, surrounded by wrinkles and a curl of grey hair. A manhole cover had been pulled aside beneath Mizuki's feet, and there, in the darkness beneath it, was Granny Murata. She was holding Mizuki's legs.

"I have got her, Josh. Quickly!"

Josh shifted the weight of Mizuki's body and let her go. She dropped smoothly straight down, and Granny pulled her into the shadows. Josh hesitated just long enough to look up into the confused and angry faces of Mizuki's stampeding fans, and then jumped down into the hole himself. He hit the cold, damp stone beneath and rolled out of the way as Jessica followed.

Granny slid the manhole cover back into place with a *clang*. Darkness closed over them and Josh sat back against the wall, gasping in air and straining his eyes to take in their new surroundings.

The wall curved up behind him, forming a stone tunnel that stretched away into the dark. Above him, the tiny holes in the manhole cover let in just enough light that he could make out Jessica bent over and panting, Mizuki slumped against the opposite wall, and a tall patch of blackness that had to be Granny Murata.

Josh tried to get to his feet. He could feel his body catching up with his brain. His calf muscles and his right eyelid were all twitching, and his throat felt scratched and fuzzy.

"Wow," Jessica rasped. "And we thought Kiki's fans could be a bit nutty!"

Josh nodded. Compared to this, even their pop star friend Kiki Chiba's craziest fans suddenly looked pretty tame.

"Mental," he gasped. "I mean *comic-book* mental. I mean like *Doctor Insano* mental."

"Thanks, *Obaasan*," Jessica bowed shakily to Granny Murata. Josh copied her, although it made fluorescent spots dance in front of his eyes.

"How did you know where to find us?"

"We heard there was a disturbance by the park. Nana's surveillance cameras did the rest."

Josh staggered over to Mizuki.

"Are you okay?" he asked. Mizuki groaned and rubbed her eyes.

Granny reached into a concealed pocket and pulled out a long black cylinder – a torch, Josh realized.

"Here," she said, handing it to Jessica. "We're in an old abandoned drainage system. If you follow this tunnel and take the first left, you will find a service ladder into the parking garage under the Sakura Apartments."

"Aren't you coming?" Jessica asked. She flicked a switch and the torch came on. It was so bright after the darkness of the tunnel that Josh had to shield his eyes.

"I have some business to take care of," said Granny.

She turned and jogged away down the tunnel, disappearing into the shadows.

"Who...was that?" Mizuki muttered. "Wearing a... a kind of mask..."

Josh glanced at Jessica. "Who?" he said, wiggling his eyebrows into the torch beam, "A mask? I didn't see anyone, did you, Jess?"

"Nobody," Jessica said. "Perhaps you hit your head? Come on." She pointed the torch down the tunnel as Josh helped Mizuki to her feet. "It's not far now."

Chapter Two

Josh leaned over the edge of the hospitality box, grinning. Ahead of him, a giant red and white Japanese flag was flying over the octagonal martial arts cage in the centre of the Nippon Budokan. Thousands of spectators filled the huge stadium, coloured scarves draped around their necks. The benches surrounding the cage were about to be filled with martial artists who'd gathered from all over the world, fighting in one of the most epic tournaments Japan had ever seen – and the Muratas had VIP seats.

Josh let out an excited sigh. *Being a ninja spy has its rewards, all right!* Since discovering Granny Murata's secret life, Josh and Jessica had been given the honour of joining Team Obaasan and helping in their fight against some of Japan's toughest crime bosses. There was only one condition: that their parents never find out. But they were busy working in Africa with *Médecins Sans Frontières*; Josh and Jessica would never share the secret.

"Ooh, Josh, look," Jessica said. Josh turned to the seats behind him where Jessica and Granny were already getting comfortable. The box was plush and high-tech, with eight large reclining chairs.

Jessica had a tall glass of lemonade in the drinks holder in the armrest of her chair. She tapped at a panel set into the other armrest. "These seats have their own TV screens!" she said. She pressed a button and a small screen unfolded from the armrest with a soft *whirr*. Writing flashed up in English and Japanese characters: *Welcome to the Ultimate Tournament, raising money for the new Tokyo Sports Academy.*

Josh sank into his own chair, booted up his screen

and flicked through the menu. He could access statistics on all the fighters, alternative camera angles on the ring, as well as sports news…

Mizuki's name caught his eye, and he tapped on it. Her face appeared on screen, with rolling English subtitles below. She still looked a little pale, but she was smiling and talking into a row of microphones. Behind her, a big window looked out over the new Tokyo Sports Academy at Edo Onsen, near the ocean. Josh could make out tall, shining apartment buildings, low, traditional slate-roofed training halls, and a running track. A faint spiral of steam rose from the hot natural springs that the brilliant new sporting facility had been built around. The whole Japanese athletics team, including Mizuki, were at Edo Onsen preparing themselves for the World Athletics Championships, which were to begin in just a few days' time.

"I am very thankful to all of my fans for their concern," Mizuki's subtitles read. Jessica leaned over to watch Josh's screen. "It is disappointing that I could not continue with the Fun Run. But I'm sure that bathing in the natural spring waters here at the Academy will help me recover in time to win a gold medal for Japan at the World Championships!"

Applause could be heard from the audience of reporters and camera crews, and Mizuki blinked as a storm of flashbulbs went off, capturing her smile.

"She's so cool," Jessica sighed. "And I can't believe she got us tickets for this fund-raiser! I know we helped her out, but this is going to be like...like..."

"Like nothing we've ever seen!" Josh lowered his voice. "Well – outside of Team Obaasan's training sessions, I mean!" They hadn't told Mizuki about their involvement with Team O and her memories of their escape were so foggy that she had no recollection of their granny appearing in a drain hole below her feet! All Mizuki knew – and all she needed to know – was that two kind twins had helped her. If she wanted to show her gratitude by getting them prime seats at the stadium, well, who were they to say no?

Josh glanced across at Granny, flashing her a secret smile. But Granny wasn't paying attention to their chatter. She was reclining in her seat and staring into the distance. The deep shadows under her cheekbones and the faraway look in her eyes made her seem even older than she really was. A stranger might've mistaken her for a tired old lady with no interest in the martial arts tournament – but Josh could read the tension in her shoulders, even under the wide folds of her silk kimono. Her fingers were drumming on the armrests of her chair.

"*Obaasan?*" Josh asked.

"Hmm?" Granny Murata's head snapped around. "Is something the matter, Josh-kun?"

"No...I was just wondering if there's been any progress on the missing scientists."

Granny shook her head slowly. "None. It's deeply puzzling."

Josh frowned. Three of Japan's most eminent pharmaceutical scientists working on some high-profile medical research at Tokyo University had gone missing several days ago and no one seemed to know why. Even Team O had no leads on what had happened to them. Josh thought of his parents, spending the summer in Africa working with *Médecins Sans Frontières*. It made his heart warm to think of them taking care of sick and injured people, giving out cures and vaccines, even doing surgery – but he knew they needed scientists like Doctor Maeda, Doctor Harada and Professor Ito to be researching better cures for the deadly diseases they were fighting.

"And...how about your other enquiries?" Jessica asked.

Granny simply rolled her eyes and shook her head.

Josh knew what they both meant: the investigation into the Yakuza crime boss, Yoshida Noboru.

"He's been so quiet lately, even after we humiliated him over the World Cup thing –" Jessica broke off to raise her hand and Josh met it in a brief high five, – "that's definitely suspicious, right?"

Granny was about to answer her, but just then the door to the box opened and a cacophony of popping camera flashes spilled in. Josh felt a huge grin spreading across his face as he saw a young woman wearing skinny jeans and a floaty purple shirt, holding hands with a young man in jeans and a Team Japan football jacket.

"Kiki! Shini!"

"Muratas!" Kiki Chiba turned her back on the flashing cameras and spread her arms. Jessica leaped up and gave Kiki a hug. "It is fabulous to see you here," she said. Josh stood up and shook hands with Shini Hanzo, the international football star and Kiki's boyfriend. As soon as the twins let go, Kiki's hand slid back into Shini's. Josh could feel Jessica shifting on the spot, trying not to actually break into a dance of joy.

"It's amazing. I still can't believe you two are holding hands in public now!" She giggled.

"We thought it was about time everyone knew we were together," Kiki said, glancing at Shini from under her eyelashes.

"Since we have no intention of being apart," Shini added with a grin. Josh glanced back at Granny – he thought he saw her expression soften into a smile, but it was gone again as soon as she saw him looking.

Suddenly all the lights started to dim, and the four of them slid into their seats as a tall man in a tuxedo stepped into the middle of the ring. The crowd applauded as he raised a microphone and started talking in Japanese, too fast for Josh to keep up. From the way the crowd's cheering swelled and died away he guessed that the announcer was giving a dramatic introduction to the first round of the men's tournament. Josh caught the words "Nippon Budokan" – the name of the stadium, which meant Japanese Martial Arts Hall – and he managed to make out that the announcer was delighted to welcome some of the best martial artists in the world…

At that moment they started to file out from a hidden backstage door: a long line of men in shorts or white martial arts uniforms, some plodding like rhinos with massive muscular chests thrust out, and others lithe-looking and dancing on the spot as they took their places around the octagonal cage.

Josh cycled through the menu on his inbuilt screen again and found the list of competitors, peering down to match the stats to the men he could see below. He knew quite a few of the names – there was the famous karateka Hideki Inoue, and Josh's heart leaped when he saw rival kung-fu champions Harry Fong and Tony Masters shaking hands as they sat down.

"Oh *wow*!" Josh gasped, as a pair of identical blond giants strode into the arena. One of them raised his hands, waving to the crowd with black Mixed Martial Arts gloves on the ends of arms that looked wider than Josh's whole body. "It's the Cooper twins!" Josh didn't need the stats to recognize the two Californians – at only twenty they were already legends in their field.

"Chad and Brad Cooper, heavyweight MMA and wrestling champions. If you put them together, they'd weigh about a quarter of a tonne!" Shini said, reading from his own armrest screen.

"It's really good of them to donate their time to this fund-raiser," Josh said. He watched Chad's and Brad's muscles ripple as they bumped their chests together. "They earn *serious* money from their fights in America."

"I wonder why they're in Japan," Jessica said.

Josh saw that Jessica's journalistic instincts had kicked in and she was scribbling fast into her notepad, taking down a description of the scene and some of the competitor stats. Great idea! He'd been meaning to practise sketching some action poses – a manga artist could never have enough practice. Before becoming members of Team O, Josh and Jessica had had other dreams for their futures – Jessica wanted to be a journalist and Josh was constantly sketching manga comic strips. When they weren't fighting crime, they still kept up their hobbies.

Josh reached into his bag and grabbed his sketchbook and a pencil just as the tuxedo-wearing announcer called out, *"Dai-ichi sentō!* Brad Cooper *tai* Chris Khang!"

Josh's pulse started to race as the two fighters stepped into the ring. How would the super-strong but slow wrestler cope with the quick, tactical fighting style of Khang, the Korean tae-kwon-do champion?

The two men faced each other across the cage and the referee, in a black T-shirt and black gloves, raised his hands between them. Josh threw down a lightning-fast sketch of the opponents, mapping out their different stances and builds with a couple of sketchy lines: Brad's intimidating lean forwards versus Khang's poised, straight-backed ready stance; the Korean's lean, taut musculature versus the American's mountain range of sweaty, pink flesh.

The referee yelled "Fight!" and stepped back to the edge of the cage. Khang sprang forwards with a cry. He leaped into a series of swift, vicious flying kicks: *thwack, thwack, thwack!* The sound of his feet striking Brad's face and neck rang across the arena, and Josh heard Kiki and Shini draw in hissed breaths of sympathy for the big man.

But Brad Cooper didn't move a single oiled muscle

– Josh didn't think he'd even *blinked* – until Khang's feet hit the floor and he was regaining his balance. Then, with a throaty growl and the power of a speeding train, Cooper charged across the cage and bore Khang to the ground, grabbing his leg and twisting it under him. The Korean fighter was flattened under Cooper's unstoppable bulk and Brad wrapped his huge thighs around Khang's until Khang was caught in a totally unbreakable leg lock.

Josh tried to sketch the tangle of limbs as they wrestled for a few seconds on the floor. It was clear that the fight was over. Brad's hold was brutal, twisting his opponent's knees in a really unnatural direction. Cooper's massive legs might as well have been made out of marble for all the chance that the Korean fighter would free himself.

Khang went limp and put an arm out, slapping his hand on the canvas. The referee raised a hand over his head to stop the match and signalled for Brad to let go of Khang.

"Submission!" shouted the announcer. "Chris Khang taps out – Brad Cooper wins! Cooper *shōrisha*!"

Josh dropped his pencil and clapped. The whole

crowd was applauding, amazed at just how quickly it was all over. Josh glanced at Granny, who sniffed and applauded politely.

I guess the brute force approach isn't quite Granny's style, Josh thought.

He watched the ring, waiting for Cooper to leap up and take his applause, but Brad wasn't moving. He still had Khang trapped in the same painful leg-lock. Khang tapped the mat again, harder, seven or eight times – but Cooper didn't move.

"Are they stuck?" Kiki asked.

She smiled, obviously joking – but Josh didn't think this was a joke, and neither did the referee. He yelled and gesticulated at Brad, and then he dived in and seized the American's huge shoulders, grabbing handfuls of muscle – but Cooper *still* didn't let go. Khang twitched, like a trapped animal. On his armrest screen Josh could see a close-up of Khang's face, pale and sweating, as if the blood was draining out of him.

"I don't believe it," Jessica breathed, sitting up very straight in her chair. "He's going to break Khang's leg!"

The applause died away and for a sick moment all Josh could hear was the grunting fighters, the ref shouting in machine-gun-rapid Japanese, and the sound of Khang's hand slapping on the mat, still desperately trying to tap out.

Josh got to his feet and leaned on the edge of the hospitality box, his heart hammering along with Khang's tapping.

"Let go!" he yelled.

In a second, the whole crowd was on its feet, booing and shouting. Four men in black T-shirts and MMA gloves stormed the ring and fell upon the two fighters, trying to prise them apart. After a tense moment, Brad released his grip and got to his feet, raising his hands as if to accept his applause, totally ignoring the fact that the referee was trying to yell at him and the entire arena was booing.

The only person still cheering was Brad's brother Chad, who was punching the air and yelling as if his twin was some kind of hero.

Beside Josh, Granny sighed and shook her head.

"The boy has no understanding of the true essence of martial arts," she said darkly.

Josh had to agree – but watching Brad lumber out of the arena with his thick head held high, he had to wonder if knowing the true essence of martial arts would be all that important if he ever found himself up against a Cooper twin.

As Josh was wondering, he heard a voice behind them ask politely: "Any concessions, sir, miss? *O-kashi*, *Obaa-sama*?"

I know that voice, Josh thought. *And it's not usually selling sweets*. He turned to see an elderly lady standing just outside the box with a tray strung around her neck, holding sweets, ice creams and drinks. Her hair was cut in a neat black bob and she was wearing a Nippon Budokan uniform. Josh recognized Sachiko, Team Obaasan's disguise expert. She gave Josh a quick wink, and then pretended she hadn't seen him.

"What a good idea," said Granny, rising from her seat. "I shall buy treats for everyone." She went over to Sachiko and they bent their heads together. Josh tried to listen, but their voices were barely more than a whisper over the excited hum of the crowd. He glanced at Jessica, and Josh saw a hint of a smile twitch across her lips. They both knew what this meant: Team O must have something urgent and top secret to tell Granny!

Down below there was a gasp from the crowd as Brad's twin Chad Cooper started the next fight by grabbing his opponent's neck and throwing him to the floor. Chad twisted, incredibly fast for someone that big, and wrapped his legs around the Muay Thai fighter's shoulders, trapping his arm between his massive thighs in a brutal arm bar. He was pulling much too hard – Josh winced as he imagined the arm popping right out of its socket. His opponent struggled painfully for a very long minute, and then managed to get his other hand free to tap out. As soon as he had, the crowd started baying for Chad to let go – but it looked like bad behaviour ran in the family.

As the deputy referees rushed the ring again, Granny came back into the box and placed a bag of yellow sweets on her armrest. She frowned down at the chaos in the ring, her lips going very thin and white, and then she tutted sharply and turned to Josh.

"I must step outside to make a telephone call," she said. "I will return shortly."

Josh shifted in his seat, itching to follow her out and see what Sachiko's news had been. But it'd look pretty odd if he just trailed after her...

"Excuse me, Mikiko-san, Shini-san?" A woman in a neat grey suit with a red laminated pass around her neck and a large camera in her hands had slipped into the box as Granny left. "*Sumimasen*, please forgive me for interrupting – could I possibly get a few photos for the Sports Academy website?"

Kiki and Shini smiled sweetly and nodded.

This was their chance. Josh tugged on Jessica's sleeve, made a telephone hand sign next to his ear and nodded towards the corridor. Jessica gave a stealthy thumbs up and they sidled out while Kiki, Shini and the photographer were occupied.

Granny hadn't gone far. With so much drama going on in the ring, all the other spectators were glued to their seats, so the concourse behind the boxes was deserted. Granny was standing beneath a large banner appealing for donations to the new Sports Academy, talking quietly into her mobile in swift Japanese.

"*Hai*," she said. "In the stadium car park in five minutes. *Wakarimashita – hai*." She saw the twins coming towards her. "*Shitsurei itashimasu*," she said, and hung up. "Now, Josh-kun, Jessica-chan," she began.

"Granny," Josh said, "before you say anything – we know something serious is going on. Sachiko wouldn't have come here if it could wait."

Granny Murata looked down her nose at Josh, and he felt a really strong urge to apologize – but he barrelled on, trying to ignore the fact that he could see Jessica giving him a warning look out of the corner of her eye.

"We want to help," he continued. "You can't even think about leaving us out of this – we've proved we can handle ourselves and whatever's happening we want to help take care of it. We're part of Team O now, remember?"

Granny sniffed, and then her wrinkled cheeks twitched into a smile.

"You are right, Josh."

I am? Josh wanted to burst into a grin but managed to keep his face under control and give Granny a respectful bow instead, even though his pulse was racing.

"But remember, your priority is your own safety – your parents must never know."

"Oh, totally," said Jessica. "They can continue

doctoring in Africa without worrying about us. We'll make sure of it. What happens in Japan, stays in Japan!"

"Hey, guys," said a voice. Josh turned to see Kiki poking her head out of the doors. "It is getting so exciting, the referee brought in two *more* deputies – are you leaving?"

"There's, erm—" Josh smiled, but he could tell it looked pretty awkward. "There's somewhere we kinda have to be..."

"It's...family stuff," Jessica said. Josh saw her eyes flick up to Granny and back again.

Kiki's face flooded with recognition. "Ohhh..." she said, and then clamped her mouth shut and mimed locking it and throwing away the key. She straightened up and gave the twins a little salute and a big grin. Josh smiled back – Kiki might not be the most subtle person on the planet, but even though she'd found out their secret when they'd rescued her from being kidnapped by Yoshida, she had never told a soul. "Good luck!" she whispered, giving them a thumbs up, and then ducked back inside.

Chapter Three

"Boooooo!"

The sound of one of the Cooper twins delivering another shockingly brutal beat-down followed Josh, Jessica and Granny down the concourse. The crowd started chanting, "*Cooper hikiage! Cooper hikiage!*" but the echo of the announcer's voice told Josh that Brad Cooper had just won, again.

"So what's going on, *Obaasan*?" Josh asked Granny as she led them down a flight of steps towards the arena car park. "Have you got a lead on the missing scientists?" Even the excitement in the stadium couldn't make him forget Team O's main priority – to solve the latest mysterious crime in Tokyo.

"Not as such," said Granny. "However, we've been watching places where we think the scientists may be taken to if they've been kidnapped and may be moved out of the country, like the airport and the docks. And Nana-san's surveillance web has picked up absolutely nothing from the docks all day."

Josh looked at Jessica, in case she understood why this was a bad thing, but Jessica's nose wrinkled up and she shrugged. "So…nothing's going on there?"

"On the contrary," said Granny, pausing at the door to the arena to fish her car keys out of the small silk handbag attached to the belt of her kimono. "Our surveillance picks up all the information that passes through telephone wires, mobile phone signals and wireless internet in that area. If we hear nothing, what does that mean?"

"It means…all those things are down?" Josh suggested. "Is it…sabotage?"

Granny nodded sharply. "I think so. The docks have

become a communication-free zone. If someone *has* kidnapped those scientists, it could be that they are intending to smuggle them out of the country tonight. There will be no way for anyone to call for help. That's very convenient for someone – I just wish we knew who."

Josh frowned. "Do you think Yoshida is behind this?" he asked.

Jessica pulled her journalist pad out of her pocket and uncapped her pen, ready to take notes. "Is that what Sachiko found out? Were there any clues at the docks?"

Granny hesitated. "We have no conclusive evidence that Yoshida is involved in either the scientists' disappearance *or* the lockdown at the docks," she admitted. "But he is one of the few Yakuza in Tokyo who is truly capable of sidestepping the authorities. Plus, he understands the extent of Team Obaasan's reach. If he wants to evade us this blackout is just the kind of thing he would do."

Josh could see Granny had a point – but he couldn't help wondering whether she was seeing the Yakuza boss in every shadow right now. He remembered

Yoshida's parting words, after they'd defeated his attempts to rig the Japan–England football game: *Your little troupe hasn't seen the last of me.* Could those words have been bothering Granny more than she wanted to admit?

Mimasu, Team O's technological genius, parked their surveillance van in the dockyard car park, slipping cunningly between two very similar big black vans with freight company logos on their sides. Josh and Jessica sat in the black leather chairs in the back of the van, beside the bank of surveillance equipment. Josh noticed that new computers had been put in the van. The TV screens that used to show CCTV footage were now touch-screen monitors displaying an interface that looked like the power grid of Tokyo.

Mr. Nakamura checked his emergency medical kit, looking for all the world like a fussy old doctor preparing for a surgery, except that he was already wearing his Team O ninja hood over his half-moon spectacles. Mr. Yamamoto stashed an amazing array of folding katanas, pop-up sai daggers and shining wooden tonfa up his sleeves. Granny opened her kimono to reveal her sleek black ninja outfit underneath. She folded the kimono into a neat square and handed it to Sachiko, who swapped it for a black hood from the disguise locker.

"Are there outfits in there for us, Sachiko-san?" Josh asked.

"Not today," said Sachiko, giving him a kindly smile.

"You will stay in the van," said Granny, pulling the hood over her head. Josh tried not to groan. Granny's eyes narrowed sternly behind the thin slit in the black hood. "You could have been seriously hurt in Yoshida's attack on the temple. You did save the football team," she said, "but you should never have been in that position. This time you will aid the team by monitoring surveillance, so Nana-san can join us on the ground."

"It is an important responsibility," Nana said, nodding encouragingly as she pulled on her own hood and tucked a stray grey hair out of sight. She picked up a pair of sleek black tablet computers. "These are Mimasu's latest invention," she said. "I've configured them to pick up every CCTV feed on the dockyard, as well as the hidden cameras we will be carrying."

"They're not affected by the signal blackout, then?" Jessica asked.

Nana gave her a long, stern look. "Do you think Mimasu would provide us with inferior technology? While the security guards can't see their CCTV images, we can!"

"Sorry," Jessica mumbled. "Of course." Mimasu was one of the best inventors in Tokyo.

Josh swiped his hand across the tablet and a map of the docks appeared, with glowing blue dots scattered across it like stars. He tapped on a group of six dots in the car park and six different video screens folded out. Three of them were black, one showed the front of the van – and two showed different views of Josh, looking down at the screen showing himself, on which there was a picture of himself...

He looked up, feeling a bit dizzy. Nana pointed to her hood, just below her right eye. Josh stared really hard, but he genuinely couldn't find the tiny hidden camera that was woven into the fabric.

"*Awesome*," he breathed.

Jessica sniggered. "Hey, I can see right up your nose!"

Josh turned away quickly.

"I've configured the tablets to pick up the audio from our microphones too," said Nana, "and you'll be able to talk back to us through them."

Mr. Nakamura leaned over to run a wrinkled finger across the screen of Josh's tablet.

"We'll be taking this route, through the fence here, over the roof of the security office and down this row of containers." He pointed to a long corridor of huge metal boxes that led to the water's edge. "We'll check these, then board this ship, which will set sail first thing in the morning, and investigate the cargo that has already been loaded. If the scientists are being smuggled out of the country on it, we need to find them before it departs."

"Ready?" Granny asked. Sachiko passed around the last of the black hoods and Team O pulled them on and gave Granny five wrinkly thumbs ups.

Jessica got up and slid open the back door of the van.

"Good luck," she whispered, and all six elderly ninjas slipped out and completely vanished into the dark so quickly and quietly that Josh almost found it hard to believe they'd been standing beside him just a few seconds ago. He definitely found it hard to believe that not one of them was under sixty years old.

Jessica pulled the door closed again and then picked up her tablet.

"This is Jessica, can you hear me?"

"*Hai*," said Granny, her voice coming in slightly tinny stereo from the two tablets' minuscule speakers.

Josh watched the Team O camera view as they approached the fence, much faster than even he had anticipated. The dim shapes of cars moved past in a blur.

One of the Team O cameras – probably Mimasu's – showed a glint of black metal as she raised a sharp pair of pliers, and then they'd cut the chain-link fence and started climbing through.

Jessica curled her feet underneath her on the leather chair and switched to one of the CCTV cameras by the fence. Josh looked over to get a better view of Team O, but even though he knew they were there, he could barely make out their shapes in the shadows.

The team began to run through the docks, their cameras wavering around as they weaved in and out of the pools of light cast by street lights, looking left and right. After only a few seconds, Josh started to feel his stomach turn over. All this blurry movement was giving him motion sickness. He decided to switch to the CCTV feeds instead, and picked a camera overlooking the security office between Team O and the cargo crates.

"Hey look," he said, showing his tablet to Jessica. "I can see the security guard. He's really bored!" The camera looked straight through the window at a man in uniform at a desk, his chin rested on one hand, staring at a bank of blank monitors.

"Well, *he'll* never spot Team O," said Jessica. "Look, there they go!" She showed Josh a view of the office roof. The darkness shifted slightly, but no more than it would do if a cloud passed over the moon.

"If we had ninja outfits, we could learn to be invisible too," Josh said, trying to fill his voice with the sound of pure innocence.

"It takes a little more than a black hood to be a real ninja," whispered Granny from her place on the roof.

Jessica rolled her eyes at Josh and he shrugged. *Worth a try, right?*

He selected a camera further down his screen, near to the place Mr. Nakamura had said their target containers would be. Towering lines of identical blocky shapes formed a wide avenue with turnings on both sides and street lights at regular intervals. The area was totally deserted. The things at the side of the road were massive metal storage crates, stacked five or ten high and extending into the distance as far as he could make out. This was just one of the huge stacks of goods, waiting to be shipped out from Tokyo harbour. Were the scientists hidden among them? Josh shook his head. It would be like looking for a needle in a haystack.

Suddenly, Jessica clutched at his arm.

"Josh!" She leaned over and swiped at his screen.

"Hey!" he said. She called up another CCTV view that was almost exactly the same, and he was about to ask her what the problem was, when he saw the dark figures moving around in the view of the camera. They weren't anywhere near as stealthy as Team O. They were large, bulky, with helmets and visors, moving like a well-oiled machine, heading down the street of containers with military precision.

"They don't look like kidnappers to me," said Jessica.

"They're not," said Josh. The letters SAT were stencilled on the back of their helmets. "That stands for Special Assault Team. They're the Japanese equivalent of a SWAT team. They're the police!"

"Granny!" Jessica called. "Can you hear this?"

There was no answer. Josh's stomach turned over. "*Obaasan*, Mr. Yamamoto – come in, Team O, we've seen something..." Josh gripped his tablet, his knuckles turning white as some of the Special Assault Team turned around and he got a good look at the guns they were holding. Was that a *sub-machine gun*?

"They're not Yoshida's Yakuza thugs," Jessica pointed out. "That means they're on our side, right? Maybe they're here to catch him too."

"But Team O are sneaking around dressed in black, and Granny didn't mention the police. What if they think Team O are involved?" He tapped the tablet, hopefully. "Granny? You have to be careful! The SATs need to know who you are!"

Crrrrrrrcccccccckkkk! Crrrrrrrcccckkkk! The tablets' speakers fizzed with static for a few seconds, and then Josh heard Granny's voice – but his relief ebbed away almost immediately.

"Josh, repeat that...something...closer to... breaking up..."

Josh gave Jessica a look of wide-eyed horror, and saw the same expression reflected back at him from her face.

"This equipment is state-of-the-art, there's no way it should be faulty."

"Maybe the same thing that's made the wireless go down is tampering with it," Jessica said. "But...does that mean someone's tampering with it...right *now*?"

Josh's pulse started to thud in his ears. "Keep trying to get the message through!"

He started to scan feverishly through camera after camera, searching for anything that looked like it could be interfering with their signal while Jessica kept repeating, "Granny, come in, the police are here, they have guns, you could be in danger, come in, Granny..."

"Oh no," Josh said, and tipped his tablet to show

Jessica a camera angle on the main gates of the dockyard. A whole battalion of policemen, clutching freakishly enormous guns, were streaming through.

"What is going on?" Jessica breathed. "Team O work for the government – why didn't Granny know there was a police operation scheduled for tonight too?"

Josh shook his head. "It could just be...a communication fail," he said. "I wouldn't be surprised if there was some kind of paperwork mistake, and they sent two teams instead of just one."

"Yeah," Jessica said. "I mean, Team O is a state secret, and I bet there's loads of red tape, and someone just failed to keep track..."

It does sound right, thought Josh. *So why do I have such a bad feeling about this?*

The audio feed made its *Crrrckk! Crrrrcccckkk!* sound again, and Josh held his breath.

"...board the ship," said Granny. "No sign of tampering with the containers." Josh quickly switched his view to the camera on Granny's hood. She was looking at another long corridor of metal boxes, but this time he could see a tall grey railing in the distance.

They had made it to the waterside and were standing on the deck of one of the cargo boats.

"Contents appear normal," Mr. Yamamoto confirmed. Josh could just make out his shape in front of Granny. He was holding a black box, its lights flashing, against the side of one of the containers. Josh could just make out an X-ray image on the screen of the box in Yamamoto's hand.

Wheeeeeeeeooooooo crzzzzzzzkkkkckk. Josh and Jessica both flinched back from their tablets as the speakers let out a whine, like feedback from an electric guitar, and then crackled again.

Josh heard the voice – it was soft, but clear, and it didn't belong to any of Team O.

"Enjoy your time inside, Mimi," it said.

Josh knew that mocking tone.

Yoshida.

Both tablets suddenly lit up, so bright Josh had to shield his eyes for a second before he realized what was going on. Floodlights had been thrown on, all over the ship. Granny's view was bathed in white, casting harsh shadows at the feet of Team O. There was nowhere to hide. Policemen swarmed out from between the cargo containers, their massive guns raised and pointed directly at Granny.

Josh heard muffled voices shouting, *"Taiho shiteshimauzo!"*

He looked at Jessica, the tablet falling flat in his lap.

"I don't believe it," he said. "Team O are under arrest."

Chapter Four

"It was a set-up!"

Josh paced up and down the van, opening lockers and searching the bank of surveillance equipment for something, anything that could help. He didn't know what he was looking for but there had to be *something*.

"This is all Yoshida's doing. He called the police – he made them think Team O were the bad guys!"

Jessica nodded. She was sitting very still, watching

the feed from Team O's hidden cameras, looking like she was about to be sick.

"I've lost audio," she murmured. "It looks like Granny tried to talk to the police, but they didn't listen. I think they cuffed their hands and found Mr. Yamamoto's weapons..." She swallowed. "They're being marched back to the police vans now."

"Granny *has* to have a plan for this," Josh said, slamming a locker shut with a *clang*. "They're government operatives, there must be something she could say to sort this out! Like a code or something!"

"She might not even need a plan." Jessica rubbed her eyes with her fists. "Once the police officials realize they've mistakenly arrested the best crime-fighting team in Tokyo, they'll let them go. Right?" She looked down at the tablet. "Well, that's it, their cameras have gone dark. They probably had to take off the hoods."

"Why do you think Yoshida wanted Team O to be arrested? To get them out of the way, even if it was only for a few hours?"

"Could be," Jessica said. "Could be more. He and Granny go back a long way – this could be revenge for all the times she's thwarted him."

"Or dumped him," Josh added. "They had a bit of a romance once, remember?"

Jessica shook her head, letting out a hiss of breath between her teeth. "This is complicated, and it's nasty. Whatever he's planning, it's got to be big – he wants Team O out of the way for a reason. And things will start happening *soon*. He won't want to waste any time whilst Team O is locked up. What do we do?"

Josh tried to take a deep breath and shove back the panic that threatened to strangle him. "We should go and search for the scientists ourselves," he said. "They could still be on that ship."

"Too late," Jessica hissed, "there are more police and they're heading this way. We don't want them to find us."

Josh grabbed a backpack from one of the lockers and bundled the tablets inside. "Let's go back to Granny's apartment. It's safe there."

Jessica quickly scooped up two headsets, two black jackets and Granny's purse, and shoved them all into the backpack. Josh pulled it on and as Jessica turned off the van's internal lights Josh slid open the back door and hopped out.

With a last look back, the twins slipped away into the night.

Josh leaned against the wall of his bedroom in Granny's apartment.

"I'm out of ideas," he said. He turned to stare at the secret keypad hidden in the bookcase, as if he could summon the pass-code out of thin air if he concentrated hard enough. The only two numbers he'd been able to think of were Granny's birthday and their dad's, but he hadn't been all that surprised to find that neither worked. "If we get it wrong again I'm afraid it'll lock down for good or self-destruct or something."

Jessica sat down on the desk, next to the pile of Japanese history books they'd pulled out to find the keypad, and ran her hands through her hair.

"I can't believe I never asked Granny for the code!" she groaned. "I just never thought we'd need to get inside the base without one of Team O around!"

Josh sighed. There was so much down there they could use. Nana's full-on surveillance tools could tap into any camera in the city; maybe they could contact the government, tell someone important that Team O were in trouble and they needed springing from jail; and if all else failed, and they had to take matters into their own hands, there was Mimasu's workshop full of crazy James Bond gadgets, or Mr. Yamamoto's wall of ninja weapons…

But it was all buried deep underneath the Sakura Apartments, accessible only by a secret elevator hidden behind a metal bookcase door thirty centimetres thick.

"If Yoshida is planning something big, how can we fight it without Team O or any of their stuff?"

"They'll be home soon," said Jessica. "We'll just have to…wait, I guess."

Josh shook his head and walked out into the sitting room.

It was kind of strange to be on their own in Granny's apartment. The ultra traditional tatami-mat flooring, the clean modern lines and white walls, the silent sliding paper doors and low, flat furniture…it had always been a bit of a culture shock after their homely, messy house back in England. But it had never felt *cold* before. Somehow without Granny it felt like walking through a museum exhibit.

Josh sat down on the low white sofa and turned on the television. It was tuned to Granny's favourite news channel. Josh's heart jumped up into his throat when he recognized the scene behind the young journalist, who was talking into a microphone in swift and excited Japanese. She was standing by the main gate to the docks. He could see the container avenues and the huge boats in the distance.

"Jess – it's on the news!" he called, fumbling for the subtitles button on the remote. Jessica launched herself across the room and landed on the sofa just as the subtitles came on. Josh read out loud as the words scrolled across the screen:

"...elite smuggling ring, arrested while attempting to board a boat in Tokyo harbour."

Josh's shoulders sagged and he tried to breathe slowly while the reporter used phrases like "heroic sting operation", "organized crime" and "counterterrorism". It tore Josh up to see his grandma being called a smuggler. *She's fought her whole life to protect this city!*

Jessica rolled her eyes and slumped back on the sofa. "It won't just go away now, will it?"

Josh shook his head. *No, I don't think it will.*

Josh woke up to the sound of a door buzzer, loud and insistent. As he rolled off his futon and struggled to his feet, the events of last night came flooding back. Jessica and he had scraped together a late, unhappy supper from the contents of Granny's fridge – some stale tempura and a bowl each of miso soup – then they'd agreed to try and get some sleep. If they were going to help Team O, they'd need to be fresh. Shame Josh had barely managed to keep his eyes shut all night.

He met Jessica coming out of her room at the same time and they approached Granny's front door together.

"Whas?" Jessica asked, rubbing her eyes and scraping her hair back into a ponytail.

Josh shrugged. "Can't be any of Team O, they'd just let themselves in..."

He slid open the little hatch beside the door and looked at the concealed monitor. It showed a black and white image of the main door of Sakura Apartments. Two women stood there, both wearing light grey suits, and the closest one had something hanging from her hip. She moved to look directly up at the camera, and Josh fought the urge to recoil. The thing on her hip was a chunky, official-looking walkie-talkie.

"Looks like the police," Josh muttered. "Are they here to search Granny's flat?"

"I wonder if they know about us," Jessica said.

"Let's not answer it," Josh said. The screen went dark, and Josh held his breath. If they couldn't get in, would they just go away again? Maybe they needed a warrant...but maybe they *had* a warrant...

Bzzzzt. Josh let out a long breath through his teeth. This time the sound came from somewhere else in the building. Josh opened up the menu on the monitor screen and changed the view to the reception area. Sure enough, the receptionist had opened the main door and the policewomen were approaching her desk, flashing their badges.

"C'mon," said Jessica, grabbing her shoes from the rack by the front door. "I want to hear what they're saying."

Josh stepped into his shoes and pocketed the keys, then followed his twin out into the corridor.

Granny's apartment was on the second floor, one of four doors that led off a central corridor. At one end of the corridor there was a balcony with a glass lift and a staircase leading down to the left – as Josh and Jessica edged towards the balcony, they could see into the reception area. In the middle of the polished wooden floor, surrounded by lush potted plants, the receptionist at her desk was leaning forward, listening to the two policewomen.

Josh tried not to breathe and carefully moved closer to the edge of the balcony, placing one foot at a time on the wooden floor, sticking close to the wall. He strained his ears and heard a conversation going on – but they were speaking in Japanese, and he didn't dare get any closer...

Then he heard the words "*igirisujin no futago*" and shrank back quickly. Those were words he'd recognize anywhere – they meant "*English twins*".

"They're here for us!" he hissed to Jessica. "Get back!"

They half crept, half ran back along the corridor and into Granny's apartment, and Josh shut the door behind them and slid the extra deadbolt into place, as quietly as he could.

"What are they going to do with us?" Jessica gasped.

"Question us?" Josh suggested. "Granny's our legal guardian while we're here – maybe they're going to take us into custody."

"Or deport us... Josh—" Jessica grabbed his arms, her jaw slack with shock. "They might *call our parents*."

"We've got to get out of here," said Josh, pacing from the door to the sofa and back again, a tiny part of him feeling bad about walking on the tatami mats in his outdoor shoes. "If we're taken into custody, there really will be nobody who knows that Yoshida is up to something."

"Maybe this was his plan all along," said Jessica. "He wants all of Team O out of the way – including us."

Josh looked around the flat again, but he saw nothing that could help them, except...

The window. He ran over and pushed it open. There was a solid-looking drainpipe outside that ran right down to the side street below. They only had to make it down two storeys. He could do this. "We can get out this way," he said. "We have to run for it." He dashed back into his room and grabbed the backpack with the tablets and headsets in it, Granny's purse, and all the Japanese yen he had in his suitcase. It wasn't very much.

When he got back to the sitting room, Jessica was leaning out of the window, her face white.

"You can do it," Josh said. "I've seen you climb much more slippery stuff than that."

"Duh," muttered Jessica. "That's not what I'm worried about. What happens if they chase us? It's the police – they'll have cars and bikes, we won't stand a chance on foot..."

"Maybe we will," Josh said. He tried to sound optimistic but it just came out a bit squeaky. "We can't hang around here, Jess..."

Jessica turned to look at him and her eyes widened.

"Got it," she said, clapping her hands together. She disappeared into her bedroom, calling back, "Give me two seconds."

Josh climbed up on the sofa to get through the window, and winced a little as he saw his shoes leaving grey footprints on the white cotton.

He jumped as muffled voices sounded from outside Granny's front door. He heard a rattling sound, like someone pulling out an enormous bunch of keys...

Jessica reappeared, carrying two skateboards.

"Brilliant!" Josh grinned. He'd forgotten all about the skateboards – they'd bought them from a totally awesome custom shop in Tokyo when they were here last summer with their parents. Jessica passed Josh the one with a manga superhero painted on the bottom, keeping the one with the rearing black stallion.

Josh shouldered the backpack and gripped the skateboard in one hand, then climbed out of the window. He braced his feet carefully against the window ledge, keeping his muscles taut until he could reach across and get a good grip on the drainpipe. He tugged on the metal bars holding it to the side of the building, and they seemed solid. He shuffled across to the end of the ledge, put one foot out, took all his weight on his hand and swung over until he was hugging the pipe.

"Here we go!" Josh said, and he let go of the metal bar. He slid down the pipe, bricks blurring in front of his face. He tried to slow himself a bit, clamping the pipe between his knees and elbows, and managed to hit the ground with a smack, rather than a crash.

He got out of the way quickly as Jessica came down after him.

"Can you believe Granny forbade us to ride these skateboards in the street because it was *too dangerous*?" he asked, as she reached the bottom. "Now, we're fighting crime with her!"

Josh gave the ground behind him a kick and the skateboard leaped forwards along the pavement. He pounded the ground a couple of times with his foot, tucking his hands behind him and keeping his knees bent for minimum wind resistance and maximum control. They turned out of the side street onto the main road, and Josh glanced back to check Jessica was with him. She was right on his tail, her ponytail whipping behind her...

And behind that, there were the two policewomen in grey coming out of the front door of the Sakura Apartments. One of them pointed, shouted something, and the other one grabbed the radio from her hip.

With a groan of frustration, Josh twisted back to look where he was going, and put on an extra burst of speed.

"Coming through!" he yelled, as the skateboard sliced along the pavement. He had to swerve to avoid a group of people coming out of one of the shops. Ahead of him a woman saw him and dropped her bag, spilling fruit all over the pavement – he had just a split second to flip up his skateboard, stomping down on the tail so that it leaped into the air and soared over the rolling melons and oranges.

"Careful, Jess," he shouted, not daring to look back.

"I see it – 'scuse, *sumimasen*, watch out!" he heard Jessica shout behind him.

Josh heard the long, slow moan of a police siren, and skidded down a side street, waving his arm over his head for Jessica to follow him.

"We've got to keep to the backstreets," he called

back, when they were both speeding down towards the little kabuki theatre. "There'll be fewer people to crash into!"

"Agreed!" Jessica shouted.

Josh put out his arm and used a street light to swing himself around another corner, catapulting himself across the road into a long residential street where the only obstacles were potted plants at the entrances to the tall apartment buildings that towered over them on both sides. He pushed the skateboard harder and then crouched, barrelling down the street like a Tokyo bullet train off its rails.

He could still hear the police siren, somewhere to his right, but he knew if they could just get a little way away and find somewhere to lie low, they'd be able to wait it out, and then...

He swerved into the road to avoid a pile of bin bags and a previously hidden intersection opened up in front of him... A police car turned the corner, coming straight towards him. It was close enough for Josh to see the policeman inside spot him and gasp before slamming on the brakes and the siren.

Josh couldn't stop. His brain went into overdrive as

the car skidded closer. *I'm not just going to get caught by the law – I'm going to skate right into it!*

Josh sped up, keeping his head down, his back foot pounding on the pavement. His eyes scanned the road, judging and re-judging the distance between the car and the skateboard...

He kicked down on the tail of his board, leaving the ground with a clatter, his wheels spinning madly in the air as he abandoned gravity and soared right over the police car, its lights flashing below him. The back wheels of his skateboard hit the boot of the car as he came down with a *clang* and he used the bounce to spring forwards another metre or so before he came down on the road on the other side of the car.

There was a shout of angry Japanese and the sound of plastic wheels skittering over the pavement, and then Jessica pulled up next to him, still gaining speed.

"Show off!" she yelled over the wind rushing past his ears.

They turned a corner together, leaning into the curve like pro skaters, and Josh stared down at the road, a broad grin spreading over his face. They were at the top of a steep hill, a street that sloped down towards a row of trees. On the other side of the park, Josh could see a wide street that held some of Tokyo's poshest houses, full of rich businesspeople and celebrities. He turned to see if Jessica had spotted it too, and she grinned at him.

There was just one more safe place they could go.

Chapter Five

"You guys," Kiki Chiba said, stacking Josh's empty noodle bowl on top of Jessica's, "I just can't believe this is happening."

Josh and Jessica nodded in sync, leaning on the funky blue kitchen counter. An hour ago, they'd been cheered up by the fact that the house Kiki had recently moved into was one hundred per cent awesome, like a mad cross between a plush European mansion, a fifties American diner and a Japanese mall. It had neon signs, silk cushions, cute manga murals and cutting-edge technology everywhere you looked. But Josh's cheer was quickly melting away under the blowtorch of their crazy situation.

"It's going to be okay," Jessica said, though her voice was flat and she was still resting her chin on her hand. "It'll all get cleared up soon – it has to."

Kiki frowned, her big brown eyes staring hard down at the counter. Josh almost wished she wouldn't – it was bad enough that Granny was in jail, they were on the run and Yoshida was planning some huge scheme...he wasn't sure he could stand it if the ultra-perky Kiki started getting all sad as well.

"What are you going to do?" Kiki asked, clearing the noodle bowls into her dishwasher. "Can I help? You can stay here as long as you need. I have many, many rooms. And money – if you need money, you tell me, okay?"

"Thanks, Kiki," said Josh, managing a smile. "You're the best. But what I really want right now is to know what Yoshida is up to."

"The Yakuza boss?" Kiki dropped one of the chopsticks and it clattered across the floor. "The one who kidnapped me? What's he done now?"

"We think he's behind Team O getting arrested," Jessica explained, tracing a pattern of stars on the worktop.

"And it may be that the police coming to Granny's apartment was part of his plan," Josh added. "I think he wants us all out of the way so he can pull off something so criminal he had to put Granny in jail to get away with it."

"All we managed to save from Team O's kit were these tablet computers," Jessica said, pulling one out of the bag and switching it on. "I know Mimasu installed a bunch of hacking apps on them, but I don't know how that'll help us find out about Yoshida's plans if we don't even know where to begin..."

Josh sighed. "We have to stop Yoshida – and soon! I just wish we could ask him what he's planning."

"Maybe you could? Is there a way we can track him down?" Kiki asked, leaning over to take a look at the tablet. "Maybe you could tail Yoko Yay and see if they meet up?"

Something went *click* in Josh's mind. Yoko Yay was Yoshida's granddaughter, the *seriously bad* pop singer, who'd been all set to steal Kiki's fabulous new TV presenting job when Yoshida had kidnapped Kiki.

"Do you know how Yoko's doing these days?" he asked Kiki. "Is she getting much work?"

"Are you kidding? I don't think she's had a real job in months."

"So, that record she put out…"

"What…'Bananas in the Sunshine'?" Jessica asked, her cheek twitching as if she couldn't quite say the words without physical pain. "That total train wreck?"

"I bet Yoshida must have paid to produce it. He must have paid for the studio, the video…" Josh remembered the video, with a bikini-clad Yoko sitting in a pile of bananas, and shuddered. "And, bad as it was, that's not criminal activity or anything, so maybe there's a chance that his real details, his address, would be on the contract?"

"It has to be worth a try," Jessica said, minimizing the CCTV display on the tablet and tapping a couple of buttons. "Let's see if we can find those hacking apps on these – it could take a lot of digging, but I *bet* we could find that contract." Josh pulled out the other tablet and opened up another window.

"Sounds like hard work. I'll make us some smoothies," Kiki said. "You'll need to keep your brain energy up. What flavour would you like?"

"Anything but banana," Josh and Jessica chorused.

"I'm really not sure about this," Jessica said, trying to cling onto the tree branch without dropping the tablet.

"We don't really have a choice," said Josh, pulling himself up onto the branch below her. He tried not to look down – they'd made it up here; there was no point dwelling on how hard they'd hit the pavement outside Yoshida's mansion if they fell.

He raised the binoculars he'd borrowed from Kiki to his eyes. They were only standard birdwatching ones, but from his vantage point in the tree they helped him to see over the five-metre brick wall and into the grounds of Yoshida's palatial home. He remembered the trick Granny had taught him: he noted the locations of all the CCTV cameras and then laid a mental filter over the top, imagining coloured circles extending about three metres for each one, and then looked for the gaps between the circles. There were very few, but...

"I think there's a path," Josh said. "If I'm right about the way that camera to the right of the fountain is pointing, I think we can make it."

Jessica shifted so she was sitting a bit more comfortably on the branch and could rest the tablet on her knees. "Okay, I'm seeing cameras on the other end of the patio, but..." There was a pause while she checked out the CCTV feeds, and Josh held on tight to his branch.

C'mon, Yoshida, give us this one...

"Yes! We're in," Jessica said. "There's a corridor of blind spots running right over the lawn – we need to get over the wall in the south-west corner, just to the right of that lamp post."

"Brilliant!" Josh reached up for the tablet and Jessica passed it down to him to slip into the backpack.

"Now we just need to climb the sheer, five metre wall," said Jessica.

"It's going to have to be The Chain. But we can do that one now. Piece of cake," Josh said, slipping his feet into the footholds in the bark and starting to climb down the tree. Jessica climbed down after him.

The twins kept close to the wall as they ran, half-crouching, towards the south-west corner of Yoshida's estate. Jessica carefully took three paces past the lamp post and stopped.

"Right here," she said, gazing up at the wall. Josh had to admit, from this angle, it did look a little more intimidating than he'd expected. He put his back against it and laced his fingers together. Jessica put one foot up into his hands and took a deep breath.

"On three," Josh said. "One, two, *three*..." He braced, took her weight, and then lifted with all his might as she stepped up into his hands and then sprang. His hands felt like two tonnes of foot had just hit them, but he pushed up, tugging against the muscles in his arms and his wrists that tried to stop him. Then suddenly all the weight was gone. He looked up, half-expecting Jessica to come tumbling down on top of him – but her feet were hanging there, a little way over his head.

Josh winced. She'd barely caught the top of the wall; she was clinging on by her fingertips.

"Don't let go! I can try and give you another boost," Josh said, but Jessica's ponytail swung from side to side as she shook her head.

"Nurf," Jessica groaned. Josh could almost see her back muscles straining through her jumper as she dragged herself up in a painful-looking chin-up until she was able to throw her arms over the brick wall and cling on more tightly. "Okay," Jessica called down. "I'm ready."

"Sure?" Josh asked. After all, last time they'd tried this she'd lost her grip, he'd bashed his tailbone really badly on the dojo floor, and then she'd fallen on his head.

"Won't be like last time," Jessica said. "At least if you keep still. Go for it."

Josh backed away and threw himself into a sprinting run-up, launching himself off the ground at the last minute and grabbing Jessica's legs just under the knees.

"Oof!" Jessica groaned, but she didn't let go of the wall. They hung there together for a few seconds, and then Jessica started to move – she inched forwards and up, tipping herself slowly over the top of the wall.

Josh clung on for dear life as he started to rise away from the ground, and concentrated hard on the bricks in front of him, resisting the urge to try to push himself up with his feet – it would only pull harder on Jessica's knees. As they'd found out last time.

Finally, with a last *"Uhn!"* from Jessica, Josh could reach to throw his arm over the top of the wall and take his own weight. Jessica lay over the wall on her stomach, getting her breath back, while he pulled himself up.

"It worked!" Josh gasped. They were in!

Chapter Six

"Woo," said Jessica. "You can be the top link next time." She wiped away the sweat from her forehead with her sleeve, and then rolled over and dropped lightly down into Yoshida's garden. Josh followed her, bending his knees as he hit the soft earth behind a bush covered in blue and white flowers.

Josh peered out between the flowers and checked the locations of the cameras. Yoshida's garden was as huge and luxurious as his house. It was dotted with flower beds, tall pampas grasses, gently trickling fountains, rock gardens of carefully raked gravel, and loads of CCTV cameras. There was one on a tall pole by the fountain over to their right, and one on each side of the wide patio on the back of the house. He drew up the coloured circles in his mind again.

"I think we've got...about three metres. Agree?" he asked Jessica.

"...I think so." She nodded.

"Stay behind me," said Josh. "We should keep right in the centre of the blind spot as much as possible." They should have plenty of room – but Granny wouldn't want them to get complacent. *Then again, she wouldn't be wild about us breaking into Yoshida Noboru's house, either.*

Their path took them through one of the rock gardens and Josh went so slowly it was almost painful, twisting and turning with every step across the gravel so as not to leave obvious footprints. When they finally made it to the patio, Josh took a second to appreciate the miracle of the fact he hadn't fallen flat on his face.

They crept up to the door and Josh balled his hand in his sleeve to turn the door handle, bracing himself for the wail of an alarm.

There was nothing. The handle turned, and the door swung open without a sound. Josh looked into a huge empty room, full of sharp angles, light glinting off metal and stone. It was Yoshida's kitchen. Josh kneeled down carefully and examined the join between the door and the tiled floor inside. There was no tripwire, no obvious raised tile that could hide a pressure plate. He took a deep breath, then crawled inside. Nothing happened.

"Unless he has a silent alarm on the door, I think we're good," he told Jessica.

"If there was an intruder in his house he'd want all his security guards to know it right away," she whispered, kneeling down and following him inside. She pulled the door to, but didn't quite shut it.

Together they crawled, slowly, across Yoshida's kitchen floor towards the door into the rest of the house. It was spotless and freezing against his hands, and smelled strongly of cleaning fluids. When they reached the door, Josh put his ear to it, listening for any sign of movement beyond, then reached up and very gently pulled it open. He peered through the crack. The kitchen was at the end of a passage with a couple of traditional Japanese brush paintings hanging on the walls. The passage was empty.

"Where now?" Jessica whispered.

"There has to be some evidence in the house, somewhere..." Josh said. "He must have a study, maybe a filing system or a computer we can hack into. Something."

"Hope so," Jessica said, as Josh edged out into the corridor. At the end of the passage there wasn't another door, but it opened out into a huge living room. It looked a lot more comfortable than the kitchen – there was a plush blue carpet, several large, squishy-looking sofas in black leather, low tables with white porcelain vases on them, and a fireplace so big Josh and Jessica could both have stood inside it with room to spare.

The twins crawled up to the back of one of the sofas and sat looking around for a couple of seconds. Two whole walls, to their left and right, were covered in shelves packed with books. Just like the kitchen, it all smelled of polish and cleaning products. Josh ran his hand underneath the bottom of the sofa and it came away totally dust-free.

Jessica elbowed Josh. "Laptop!" she hissed. "On that table!"

Josh peered over the sofa. There was a laptop there, its lid open, displaying a screensaver of swirling coloured lines, a bit like the strokes of a brush pen.

After pausing a couple of seconds longer to make sure there was nobody coming, Josh and Jessica crawled out into the middle of the room and Josh gingerly tapped the spacebar on the laptop. The screensaver froze...

Don't be password-protected...don't be password-protected...

...and then the screensaver disappeared and revealed Yoshida's desktop, a landscape photograph of a mountain Josh vaguely thought might be Mount Fuji. Josh pumped the air in a silent *YES!*, and gave Jessica a quiet high five.

"No files on the desktop," Jessica whispered. "How can we tell what he did last?"

"Way ahead of you." Josh brought up the internet browser and clicked through to the search history. "Most recent searches: Armani Tokyo; fine dining, Edo Onsen."

"Well that fits," Jessica said, glancing around at the

plush sitting room. Josh scanned down the list of URLs. There were sites for ordering luxury products, listings for opera and classical music concerts in Tokyo...

And then two letters caught Josh's eye.

"Tokyo.*ac*," he muttered out loud.

"Ac? That stands for 'academic'," Jessica said, leaning over to see. "Why did he go to Tokyo University's website?"

"Not just the university," Josh said, the hairs on his neck prickling as if a cold blast of air had just hit the back of his head. "Check it out. www.tokyo.ac.jp/pharmascience."

Jessica leaned back slowly. "Woah. Josh..."

"I know. The pharmaceutical science department – where those missing scientists worked."

"Click it."

Josh did. The page that came up was a clean blue and white profile of the heads of department – Doctor Maeda, Doctor Harada and Professor Ito. Along the top ran a blue box with a short message in Japanese and English: *Tokyo University gives greatest respect to the families of Doc. Maeda, Doc. Harada and Prof. Ito, and hopes that they are returned safe very soon.*

"Why is Yoshida interested in the scientists? Do you think he really *is* behind their disappearance?" Jessica stood up, running her hands through her hair and then shaking them out, as if Yoshida's creepy scheme was making her skin crawl. "But why? What would a gangster boss want with three university professors? And where are they now?"

She started to pace across the room, deep in thought. Josh gave the internet history another glance, but there wasn't much else that looked useful.

"Hey – Josh, come here."

He closed the browser window and stood up. Jessica was by the fireplace, staring down at the floor as if there was something bizarre at her feet. Josh couldn't see what she was looking at – there was nothing there except the plush carpet.

He was just opening his mouth to ask what she'd spotted, when he saw that there were two thin indented lines in the carpet, right next to the tiled base of the giant fireplace, sticking out into the room. The fibres were all worn down and a slightly different colour, like the marks that you found under a sofa when you moved it around to clean underneath. Josh kneeled down next to the marks, careful not to disturb them, and gingerly reached out to touch them. They felt completely smooth.

"The rest of this room is so perfect," Jessica said. "It seems odd that these would've been left."

"Maybe something was here," Josh guessed. "Maybe they took something away that had been here a while, and haven't fixed the carpet yet. Something like…" He trailed off. He had no idea what would make this kind of mark, except maybe a pair of skates – but he hardly thought Yoshida would encourage skating in his living room…

"Josh!" Jessica's hand suddenly came down on his shoulder, gripping tight. "I think I heard…"

Josh held his breath and straightened his back, listening hard. There was a long moment of silence, except for a slight background hum coming from the laptop…and then Josh heard a footfall, and then another. Shoes with hard soles, on a hard wooden floor.

He looked up and met Jessica's eyes. *Someone's coming!*

Chapter Seven

They dived and hit the carpet behind one of the big leather sofas.

Someone stepped into the room.

"No, *you* listen," growled a voice in Japanese. A picture flooded into Josh's mind – an old man, wiry and strong, with a gaunt face and a thin, grey ponytail.

Yoshida, he mouthed to Jessica. She gave him a quick nod and tucked herself tighter against the back of the sofa.

Yoshida's voice went on, and then he paused, as if listening. *He must be on the phone*, Josh thought. His Japanese was complex, Josh guessed maybe old-fashioned – but there were a couple of words Josh could catch.

"*Shushō…shinkokuna juyō…*"

Prime minister…serious…demands… He thought there was something about a ransom…people dying…

Yoshida paused again, and then laughed. It didn't sound like a friendly laugh.

Josh looked up at Jessica. He thought she hadn't caught as much of it as him – she gave him a thumbs down and raised an eyebrow.

Is it bad?

He put both thumbs down and made a grave face. *Very, very bad.*

Josh itched to get a look at Yoshida's face, but he didn't dare move.

He heard Yoshida's shoes clicking on a hard surface and then a low, rumbling, grinding sound. Yoshida spoke again, but his voice sounded further away…and then it was suddenly cut off, in the middle of a sentence. Josh frowned. Had he left the room?

Josh looked down at his watch, following the second hand carefully as it ticked around. Thirty seconds…a minute…two full minutes of silence passed. Josh and Jessica looked at each other, nodded, and then stood up slowly. Josh tensed, ready to bolt if it was a trick, half expecting Yoshida to be waiting for them.

The room was empty.

"Where did he go?" Josh whispered.

Jessica grabbed his sleeve. "D'you really want to hang around here and find out?" Even as the words left her lips, there was a sudden clatter by the window and they almost jumped out of their skins. A guard dog was throwing himself at the plate glass, his lips curled back in a snarl as his eyes glared at them.

"We need to get out of here before someone comes to investigate!" Josh hissed. Jessica pulled him away towards the kitchen. They poked their heads around the kitchen door. Although the guard dog had raced round to try and find them, he strained on a leash tied to a stake, just out of reach of the kitchen door. No doubt he was tied up so that he wouldn't trip the surveillance cameras.

"Quick!" Jessica said. "Before he snaps his leash and has us for dinner." They dashed back across the blind corridor to the garden wall. Josh had never run so fast.

"You know we're going back there, don't you?" Josh said, as Jessica tapped the security code into Kiki's front gate.

"For sure," his sister agreed. "We can't just let that go. Yoshida has to be hiding something – why else would everything look so spotless and innocent in the home of a criminal mastermind? There has to be something – a hidden room, an annexe, a...*something*! – that we didn't have time to uncover."

As they walked towards the front door, Josh looked up at their friend's house. The outside was nearly as cool as the inside, with a turret bedroom and a swimming pool at the back, and...

"Wait," he said. Jessica paused.

"What?"

"It's just...it's starting to get dark, and none of Kiki's lights are on."

Jessica looked up at the house. Every window was dark. "Maybe she's gone out," Jessica said.

"On foot?" Josh asked, pointing to the sporty purple convertible parked in the driveway. "Kiki's too famous to just go for a walk, she'd cause a stampede. And if she was going somewhere with her bodyguard, she would've known in advance and she'd have waited for us to get back, or at least told us she was going somewhere."

Jessica walked up to the front door, moving quietly. She put her hand up to the polished wood...and it swung open. Metal and splintered wood glinted in the street lights. The lock had been broken off – someone had kicked their way in.

Kiki's voice broke the silence, crying out in shock, and there was a *crash* from somewhere inside the house. Josh leaped into the dark corridor with Jessica on his heels. They crept towards the sounds, moving like shadows. Another voice, not Kiki's, came from the kitchen. It was a deep gruff voice, and it barked something in Japanese and then repeated in English: "Where are the children, Mikiko!? If they are here I will find them!"

"What children?" Kiki gasped. "I don't know what you're talking about!"

Oh no. Josh's heart sank as he sidled up to the closed kitchen door. *Don't be a hero, Kiki!* If she got injured trying to protect them...he just couldn't let that happen.

"We have to save her," Jessica whispered sharply, her eyebrows drawn down in an angry scowl.

"Seriously," Josh heard Kiki whimpering through the door, "if you want money, or something, I have money, more than you would get in ransom, please, do not hurt me..."

A movement made him look at Jessica. She'd straightened up, her eyes wide, and leaned forwards as if listening intently to something behind the door... *just* behind it. Jessica looked at Josh and nodded. She drew herself back, turned and gave the door a sharp, hard side kick.

Instead of flying open it hit something solid, and someone grunted, "Oof!" Then there was a *clang* like metal hitting the tiled floor.

Josh burst through the door into the dim kitchen, squinting to make out people in the shadows, and then a big grunting shape loomed up in front of him and he ducked, feeling the air move as a punch soared over his head. He slammed both fists forwards. They connected with a satisfying *thump* right in the man's belly, and he doubled over.

Josh heard Jessica cry out, *"Hai!"* and a pair of quick *thuds* as another giant shadow moved to his right, and then fell back groaning.

"Kiki, call the police!"

"They cut the landline and took my mobile phone!" Kiki's voice said, and Josh just caught a glimpse of her, sidling around the edge of the room. "I'll go next door!"

"No, you don't," growled one of the men. Josh saw another big shape lunge towards Kiki, its arms like blunt pincers trying to grab at her. Josh threw himself into a somersault and a handspring, vaulting over the kitchen counter with a clatter of plates and cutlery. He could still barely see a thing; he didn't even know how many of them there were – but he knew if it wasn't Kiki or Jessica, he should hit hard and sort it out later.

He reached across the oven hob and fumbled along the wall till he found what he knew was there – a huge, heavy wok. He grabbed it from its hook and swung it like a tennis racquet at the dark figure leaning over the counter, trying to grab him. It hit the man's face with a cartoonish *thunnnnnng* and a *crunch*. The man fell back, hit the floor and didn't move.

Josh stepped out into the kitchen, wielding the wok like a sword in front of him – and then his arms were pinned to his sides, his chest constricted by a solid, muscular arm thrown across it.

"Stupid kid, I got you!" growled a voice in his ear, accompanied by the tickle of a beard on Josh's neck. The bear hug tightened, and Josh gasped in a breath while he still could. It felt as though the man was trying to crush Josh's ribcage. The wok was useless while he couldn't swing his arms, but his wrists were still free. Maybe…

Josh flipped the pan upwards, right at his own face, and threw his head to one side. The wok spun through the air and smacked into the guy behind him. The crushing hold loosened as his attacker bent double, clutching his nose.

"Mmnnnnffkf!" the man tried to scream. Josh wriggled out of his grip and leaped up, planting his hands on the counter to give himself a boost and thrust two kicks into the man's chest, sending him crashing back, still holding his nose. He slammed into Kiki's fridge, sending a shower of magnets skidding across the floor, and flopped face down.

Heavy footsteps sounded behind Josh, and he twisted away before the next thug could grab him. He seized the fridge door and pulled it open, ducking behind it like a shield just as a heavy fist flew through the air. The fridge light came on, illuminating a shock of curly black hair and a scarred chin, the glint of a man's grey eyes as his fist smashed into the shelf of Kiki's fridge. He pulled his hand back, covered in bits of egg and dripping with milk. Josh reached into the fridge and grabbed a huge magnum of champagne, swinging it like a club and coming down *bong* on top of the man's head. He crumpled.

In the light from the fridge, the kitchen was a bit clearer. Josh saw Jessica struggling with a man whose hair stuck straight up. She was managing to land a few hard thumps on his body although he had a firm hold on her wrist. Kiki wasn't there – she must have got out to call the police. The bearded man he'd hit with the wok was climbing to his feet, lumbering towards Josh, stepping over the legs of two of his fellow thugs. Josh shook up the champagne bottle as hard as he could and then tugged off the cork. A fountain of fizz shot out of the bottle and exploded into the man's face. He tried to wipe his eyes and keep going, but he stepped on a fridge magnet lying in a pool of champagne and slipped, falling backwards.

Nice work, he told himself, grinning.

"Jshmmmmm!" Jessica tried to cry out. Josh froze. The thug had got behind her and he was covering her face with a cloth. Her arms were going limp...

A sickly sweet, eye-watering smell hit him, and then there was something on his face.

Chloroform.

Silence fell, like a blanket being thrown over everything. He felt pressure on his back, and then everything went dark.

Chapter Eight

Josh's eyelids fluttered open.

He was lying somewhere really soft and comfortable, in a bright room. He turned his head, and found himself looking at blue sky through a large window. The air was fresh – he could breathe freely, and he thought he could smell grass – was there a garden nearby?

This is nice, he thought dozily. Then the memories came flooding back. They'd been chloroformed! Not nice at all!

He tried to sit up. His head throbbed, and everything was kind of blurry and pink-tinged even after he rubbed his eyes, but he managed to get to a sitting position and keep still until everything stopped spinning.

Eventually, the blurriness melted away and his focus sharpened. Everything remained kind of pink though.

He was in someone's bedroom, though it was at least twice as big as any bedroom he'd ever seen before. The bed was plush and squishy, with what felt like silk sheets under his hands, and it was so enormous that Jessica was lying on the other side of it, her arms splayed, and there was still about thirty centimetres of space between them. Over to his right there was a massive TV, probably wider than his arm-span, the centrepiece in an entertainment centre stuffed with DVDs, games, and on the middle shelf, controllers for at least four different kinds of games consoles.

There was a desk on the other side of the room, a polished wooden thing with scrolls and hearts carved into its surface – *maybe an antique*, Josh thought.

There was a desktop PC on it, another massive screen in front of a sleek and gleaming processing tower. There were a couple of large, framed posters from pop concerts behind it on the wall.

Josh half climbed and half fell out of the bed and onto his feet, staggering across the room – thick, squishy carpet underfoot – to switch the computer on. If he could get on the internet, maybe he could work out where he was, or get a message to Kiki – that is, if they hadn't got her too.

There was a *vrrrrummm* sound as the computer came to life, and after a couple of progress bars the screen showed a desktop littered with saved files and a background image of a kitten – but when Josh tried to open the internet, the browser just flashed up an error message: no internet connection found.

"Of course not," Josh muttered.

The picture was starting to come together. Ridiculously luxurious room, big garden outside... He knew who this house belonged to.

He went over to his sister and shook her shoulder.

"Wake up, Jess."

"No," Jessica groaned. "'S too bright. What?" She

looked around the room, slowly shifting from bleary-eyed blank confusion to sharp suspicion. "What's going on? What is this place?"

There was a soft *click* and the door swung open. A thin, straight-backed elderly man with grey hair in a long ponytail stood there, smiling almost kindly at them.

"Yoshida!" Jessica sat bolt upright, fully awake.

"Josh-kun, Jessica-chan," said Yoshida, giving a brief but graceful bow. "I hope you slept well. Is Yoko's room to your liking? She comes to stay with me when she can."

Jessica's mouth dropped open. Josh stepped forwards, his fists clenched, fighting the urge to get hysterical. *You chloroformed us! You kidnapped us! We are not your guests, you crazy old man!*

"It's not to our liking at all, actually, so if you'll just stand aside we'll be on our way," Jessica said brightly, not so much smiling as baring her teeth at the mob boss.

Yoshida chuckled, just like someone's harmless old grandad. "Very amusing."

"If you don't let us go, right now..." Josh pulled

himself up to his full height and squared his shoulders. "You're seriously going to regret it."

"Not this time," said Yoshida. The convivial smile didn't leave his face, but his eyes turned cold. "You two have been a severe nuisance to me this summer. After dear Mimi's unfortunate run-in with the authorities, I thought that the police would take custody of you. But since they seem incapable of doing their duty, I've had to step in to take care of the situation." His smile widened, like a crocodile's. "As a friend of the family."

Josh wanted to launch himself across the room and punch the smile right off Yoshida's face. Beside him, Jessica twitched.

Yoshida gave them another little bow. "You will be my guests here until it is all over."

"Until what's all over?"

"Josh, Josh..." Yoshida shook his head. "You cannot believe I am *that* stupid. When it is done, you can go. In the meantime..." He waved an arm, taking in the television and PC and the shelves of games. "There is more than enough here to keep you entertained. There is nothing in this room you could possibly use to escape but if you wish to waste time trying that is your choice. There is a bathroom through that door. My kitchen staff will bring you three meals a day. Also, the glass in the windows is shatterproof. Have a good stay."

With that, he bowed out and locked the door behind him.

"Welcome to the Hotel Yoshida," Jessica muttered. "We hope you enjoy the sense of hopelessness and thinly-veiled threat of violence."

"Don't forget the lingering scent of chloroform," Josh said. "But we have to remember – Yoshida will want to be extra-double-super-certain that nothing is going to get in his way this time."

"Which means we have to get something in his way," said Jessica. "Right now! Preferably something that comes with sirens and handcuffs."

"But how?" Josh scanned the room again, looking for something Yoshida had missed. "No phone, no internet. The windows don't open so we couldn't even make smoke signals, not that we have anything to light a fire with."

"I dunno," Jessica said. "Maybe we could reflect

the sunlight off the back of one of the Xbox discs and set the bedding on fire."

"That wouldn't..." Josh began, but he trailed off. "Wait. *Wait*." He jumped up from the bed and went over to the entertainment centre, grabbing the massive remote control and one of the Xbox controllers.

"Josh?" Jessica looked over his shoulder. She spoke slowly and softly, as if she thought he'd totally cracked. "I was kidding. I don't think we should set fire to the bed."

"Me neither." He held up the Xbox controller. "I bet Yoshida doesn't realize this connects to the internet!"

Jessica gaped at him for a moment and then raised her hand in the air. "Give me five, you utter genius," she laughed. Josh high-fived her and then turned on the television and the console. The TV was tuned to a news channel, where a lady in a suit was talking in agitated Japanese. Josh bent over the remote control, searching for the button that would switch the display to the Xbox.

He looked up as the newsreader uttered the words "World Athletics Championships" and "Mizuki".

"...The new Sports Academy at Edo Onsen, where

the Japanese athletics team is staying has been put into quarantine until the cause of the mysterious illness has been determined," the subtitles read. The screen showed a map of Edo Onsen with a big red circle around the Academy where the Japanese athletes were living and training. "We are told that the team has been bathing in the hot springs at Edo Onsen and all of Japan hopes that this will help them to a swift recovery."

"It's the whole team," Jessica said. "They've all come down with this...whatever it is. Do you think it's the same illness as Mizuki had? Can you imagine if there wasn't a single Japanese athlete at the World Championships?" She shuddered.

Josh shook his head, pushing the thoughts aside. "It has to be one of these buttons *here*..."

The newsreader finally winked out of sight and a green and grey screen popped up, with a swirling stream of coloured pixels and a harmonious background hum.

"This is it! Xbox LIVE is running – that means we can contact someone!"

"But can we call the police from it?" Jessica said.

"I don't think so." Josh scrolled through the menus. Some of them were in Japanese, but he knew the layout like the back of his hand and quickly found the login screen and tapped in his username and password. *I knew all that time I spent gaming back at home wasn't totally wasted*. His avatar popped up in the corner of the screen, a cartoon version of himself wearing a ninja hood. It waved to him. Josh was so relieved he almost waved back.

"We can contact anyone who's on the network, if we know their username," he said. "But who can we call? I mean, I could try Miles or Kat from school but I don't think they'd be a lot of help."

"We can try Kiki," said Jessica. "With a bit of luck she got out to call the police, and didn't get kidnapped too. She told me the secret name she plays under so she won't get mobbed by fans online. It's SailorMinnie."

Josh entered the name in the search box and hit *go*. "We just have to hope she's...at home," he said, a sick feeling coiling in his stomach. He held his breath while another stream of brightly-coloured pixels filled the screen, sparkling around the word *searching*.

A female avatar in a bright purple skirt and black top appeared on screen, but the profile status box said *offline*.

"Doesn't mean she's not okay," Jessica said. "If my house had been broken into I probably wouldn't be on a games console right now either. She could be at Shini's house."

"I hope you're right," said Josh, selecting a line of Japanese characters he knew stood for *Send this user a message*. "This should go straight to her email, which should go straight to her phone, so she should pick it up right away."

"That's a lot of should," Jessica muttered.

SOS, Josh typed into the message box. *Log on to Xbox ASAP. J+J.*

He hit *send* and the message vanished.

"Now we wait," Jessica said. She started chewing her thumb almost immediately. Josh found himself staring at the walls, at the garden outside the window...

"Josh, do you—" Jessica began, then broke off suddenly.

"What? Is she there?" Josh said, but Jessica put her fingers to her lips.

"Shh!" she said, and cupped her ear with her other hand.

Josh listened, and cringed away from the door as he heard footsteps on wood, walking down the corridor outside. They got louder, and louder, and stopped… and then started to get softer again, moving away. Josh breathed again.

"Probably a guard," Jessica said, softly. "We should keep it down."

"Yeah. Clearly, Yoshida's not *so* confident we can't escape that he'd risk not setting a guard," Josh muttered.

A couple of seemingly endless minutes later, the Xbox made a soft *blip* sound and Josh nearly dropped the porcelain kitten he'd picked up off Yoko's bedside table.

"She's online!" Jessica hissed.

A chat window popped up, with a message.

SailorMinnie: Jess? Josh?

Josh typed like the wind.

JMninja: We're here! Captured @ Yoshidas

SailorMinnie: ONO. U have hedset 2 talk?

Jessica scrambled to the entertainment centre and rifled through the drawers, but came up empty-handed.

JMninja: no
SailorMinnie: 2bad :(
JMninja: call cops. gonna leave Xbox on n they cn trace IP addy, shd lead them here
SailorMinnie: on it

Josh and Jessica breathed out twin sighs of relief.

JMninja: turning tv off, less suspicious
SailorMinnie: K. <3. B safe

Josh hit the off button on the TV screen. The lights on the console carried on flickering.

"Brilliant," said Jessica. "Thank goodness for Kiki! I bet Yoshida won't be happy when a bunch of police turn up on his doorstep."

"Yeah…" Josh imagined the Yakuza boss's face,

and sniggered, but the image faded quickly. "As long as they get here in time."

Josh stared out of the window. "Yoshida's been one step ahead of us all this time," he said. "He's made sure Team O are out of the picture. Whatever he's planning has to be especially diabolical. It'd be awful if the police got here too late. We can't rely on them. If he has kidnapped those scientists and something happens to them, I want to say I've done absolutely everything I can to stop Yoshida, even if it doesn't work. Otherwise, what's the point of calling ourselves secret agents?"

"You think we should get out of here and stop him ourselves? You're mad." Jessica took a deep breath. "But count me in!"

Chapter Nine

"One problem," said Jessica. "We're still locked in this room."

Josh got down on his knees and crawled towards the door, moving silently. He put his ear to the wood and listened. There were footsteps again, but they were faint – the guard must be at the far end of the corridor. Of course, that meant he'd be coming back this way soon.

Josh peered at the lock. It was like the rest of the

room, smart and clean...and domestic. This wasn't the kind of lock Yoshida would have on his most dangerous prisoners, it was the kind of lock a teenage girl would have on her door. It probably used a simple key with only a couple of teeth.

He backed away from the door, still on his knees, and then stood up and beckoned Jessica over.

"If we can get the face off, I think we can pick the lock," he whispered. "We just need to undo those screws. Look for something hard and pointy with a flat end."

Jessica nodded and they cased the room, opening drawers and searching through boxes. Josh pulled open the wardrobe and let out a breath of triumph – there was Yoko Yay's make-up bag, and if he was lucky, inside...

"Yes!" he hissed, pulling out a metal nail clipper with a flat end.

Jessica followed him back to the door and stood with her ear pressed to it while he kneeled in front of the lock. Jessica held up her hand. *Not yet*... She held completely still and shut her eyes, listening hard. Josh tried not to breathe. *Wait...wait...* Finally, she gave a thumbs up and Josh stuck the end of the nail clipper into the groove on the first screw and twisted. It made a squeaking noise that sounded deafening to Josh, but Jessica made a hand motion like winding up string. *Keep going, it's okay.*

Josh got the first screw out of the lock, and then the second. The third was stiffer, but he wrapped his hand in the end of his sleeve and gripped the nail clipper as hard as he could. The screw finally gave way and the nail clipper skittered off course, digging a groove into the wood of the door with a loud *SKRRRRITCH*.

Josh sat back, completely still. He could hear the guard's footsteps now – they were right outside the door. Had he heard the noise? The sound came closer…but didn't stop. The guard walked right past the door and off down the hall.

Josh waited for Jessica to give the sign, and then quickly took out the final screw and carefully lifted the metal panel off the lock. Once the inside was exposed, it was the easiest lock Josh had ever picked.

"Pretty sure there's only one guard. We can take him," Jessica whispered. Josh nodded. Jessica pressed her ear to the door and held up her hand, fingers outstretched. She folded them down slowly, one by one.

Five...four...three...two...

Two seemed to go on for a very long time.

One...

Josh got into a ready stance facing the door, placing his legs one in front of the other, slightly bent, relaxing his shoulders.

Jessica wrenched the door open. The guard was right outside, a burly man with a broken nose and squashed features. He turned, his eyes widening in shock, and before he could cry out Josh thrust a high kick into his face, his trainer connecting with a *thud* right between the man's eyes.

He fell forwards. Josh's heart skipped – if he thumped onto the floor, it might bring more of Yoshida's goons running to see what had happened...

Jessica's reflexes kicked in and she caught the guard, staggering under his weight. Josh jumped in and together they dragged him through the door into Yoko's room and let him fall quietly forwards onto the soft pink bed.

Jessica ran to the computer desk, pulled out some

wires from the drawer and wound them around the man's wrists and ankles. Josh tugged the man's tie up around his mouth to form a gag and tied it at the back of his head, then fished the key off his belt. Jessica screwed the lock back on the door. Pocketing the nail-clippers, she held open the door and together they slipped out into the hall, locked the door behind them and set off. Josh gave his sister a quick grin as they turned the first corner.

We're free!

Fifteen, twenty, thirty minutes passed while they explored Yoshida's house. The whole place was starting to give Josh the creeps – it was much too quiet. *But we can't leave until we've found something. Some clue to tell us what Yoshida's up to!*

Josh turned a corner. The corridor opened up into the living room they'd been in before, with the fireplace big enough for them both to stand in and the huge black leather sofas.

They crept forwards and looked inside the room. It was empty.

Jessica started across the room towards the kitchen and the way out, but Josh hesitated.

"Keep an eye out for anything," he said. "However insignificant-looking. I want to know how Yoshida got out of here without us hearing him move. And I want to know what he's hiding."

He walked carefully across the carpet, coming to a stop beside the fireplace, opposite the sofa where he and Jessica had been hiding when Yoshida vanished. "He was standing somewhere around here."

Jessica walked back to the door that led to the rest of the house. "I'll keep watch," she said. "But try to be quick. We've been really lucky so far, I don't want to push it. I guess that guard dog's still lurking outside."

"Will do," Josh said. He looked all round him, up at the ceiling and behind him at the bare wall, and then finally down at his feet. There was the strange mark on the carpet again, as if something had worn down the fibres.

That can't be a coincidence. It has to mean something, he thought. *He was standing here, we heard him speak, and then it was as if he just walked into the wall...*

Josh stepped inside the fireplace, running his hands over the back of it, and then pushed with all his might, but it wouldn't budge. It had to be something more subtle than that, something that looks right, but isn't...

Josh scanned the fireplace, looking for something that didn't seem to fit. He even tried to pick up one of the coals – but it wouldn't budge. It was a gas fireplace, the coals were fake. But if that was true, why was there a coal scuttle right beside him?

He tried to pick that up, but the pressure of his hand sent it sliding across the tiles, with a smooth oiled motion. There was a low rumble, and the entire fireplace began to move. Josh jumped back as it turned, rolling over the track mark on the floor, revealing a completely identical fireplace on the other side. A breath of cold air hit Josh's face.

"Wow," Josh said aloud. "Someone's been watching too many classic Bond films."

Jessica was watching with her mouth hanging open. "That's incredible," she said.

"Jess," Josh said, slowly, "why weren't there more guards?"

"What?"

"Seriously." Josh let his voice lift to normal speaking volume. Jessica cringed, but nothing else happened, no guards came running. "Yoshida had more guards than this on the waxworks museum, and all that was going on there was a harmless pop star was unconscious and tied to one of the exhibits. This is his *house*. It's not right."

Jessica hesitated, then abandoned her post and walked over to the fireplace. "We did wander around this place unchallenged for like three quarters of an hour."

"I have two questions," Josh said. "One: if he's planning something so huge he had to get all of Team O out of the way, us included, how come his security's so lax?"

"Because..." Jessica frowned. "He's not stupid, he must know he's not in any danger. He's confident."

"So then, question two, why is he *so* confident?"

Jessica shrugged. "I don't know."

"I do. He *knows* he can't be stopped, because whatever it is, it's happening *right now*, down there."

Jessica looked at Josh for a long moment, and then stepped into the fireplace.

"Let's go," she said, "before it's too late."

Josh got onto the fireplace beside her, and slid the coal scuttle again. The fireplace turned slowly. The sitting room slid away out of sight.

The other side of the fireplace was cool and dark. All the light from the sitting room vanished, and a breeze that smelled of old stone and wood blew past them. Then everything was still.

They were standing on a dark stone landing at the top of a flight of steps, lit with eerie black lights that made the shadows seem like a physical part of the stairs.

"Here we go," Jessica said. She placed a foot on the first step. "Ready or not."

Chapter Ten

Josh and Jessica's footsteps echoed on the stone as they descended the steps, no matter how they tried to muffle the sound. The staircase curved down in a gentle spiral around a central pillar, so even if Josh tried, he couldn't see around the corner or work out how far down they were going.

The air grew colder as they walked, and the wall began to feel slightly damp under Josh's fingers. The hum from the black lights buzzed around his head like an invisible fly.

He stopped, suddenly tense, feeling like the walls were closing in…

Don't be an idiot, he told himself. *They are closing in; the stairs are getting narrower. We must be nearly there.*

The stairs ended and a tunnel opened up in front of them. The black lights ended at the bottom of the stairs, so after a metre or so the tunnel vanished into an empty dark space.

Jessica put a hand on the wall.

"It feels like a cave," she said. "Like natural stone."

Josh felt along the wall, too. She was right. He thought he could even feel some plant life growing between two rocks. At least, he *hoped* that soft, damp thing he'd touched was a plant…

"D'you think Yoshida built this?" Josh wondered.

"I don't know – everything else in his house is so *clean*," Jessica said, peering at her fingertips. "I think this has been here a long time. Maybe longer than the house itself."

Josh shuddered. He really didn't want to know

what Yoshida was doing down here. Assuming Yoshida did go down here. But it made sense, didn't it? He surely had to have a hideout. They had no choice but to keep going. Jessica put a hand on his shoulder and they walked into the dark together.

Josh's heart felt like it might be trying to climb out of his mouth so it didn't have to come with them, but they pressed on, until suddenly a sliver of light cut through the dank air and Josh heard a murmur of voices and some electronic beeping. Josh and Jessica pressed themselves to the rough stone wall like Granny had taught them, and edged silently towards the opening. The light brightened and opened out as they approached, until their eyes adjusted. Centimetre by centimetre they crept forwards, until Josh could see through into the well-lit space beyond the tunnel. They lay down on their stomachs to crawl closer without being seen.

The chamber was enormous, like a huge natural cavern, complete with a couple of small stalactites hanging down from the ceiling.

Josh's heart sank as he took in the sight.

It was like a cross between Team O's high-tech

hideout and an ancient amphitheatre. In the middle of the room there was an empty open space about the size of a tennis court. Stretching up to their right they could see rows of benches carved into the natural stone in the shape of a semicircle, positioned to see whatever was going on down on the floor. The seating extended out of Josh's line of vision – he could only imagine how far back it went. It looked ancient, its once-sharp edges worn down over time. There were a few squat carvings at the end of the rows that looked like the ones from ancient Shinto temples, animals and demons with wide mouths full of teeth and huge staring eyes.

To their left, the ancient collided with the modern at a sheer wall that stretched up to the ceiling. A huge, multiplex-sized cinema screen took up about half the wall. Josh gulped as he recognized the picture: the new Sports Academy at Edo Onsen. An ominous red line was pulsating on the map, running in from one corner of the screen and ending right in the centre of the hot springs at the heart of the complex.

In front of the screen there was an enormous control

desk, crowded with screens, buttons, dials and levers. Three people in white lab coats sat on chairs beside the controls, just out of reach of them. A grey-haired man, a middle-aged woman and a younger man. Their shoulders were slumped, and each one was flanked – *guarded*, Josh corrected himself – by a hulking Yakuza goon in a black suit.

Professor Ito, Doctor Maeda and Doctor Harada. They're here. Josh looked again at the red line on the screen, leading to the hot springs at Edo Onsen, and his skin prickled and felt chilled against the cold stone. His glance was being drawn, almost against his wishes, across to the other side of the controls. He didn't want to look. He so did not want to be right...

A red pipe emerged from the back wall and ran down to three large tanks, bright yellow with black signs on their sides. Josh didn't need to be able to read Japanese to see that the symbols meant *danger*.

That pipe is the red line on the screen. It goes all the way to the springs at Edo Onsen. Yoshida is poisoning the Japanese athletics team.

"Mizuki," Jessica whispered, her voice barely more than a breath of air on his ear. "That's why she was ill." Josh nodded. Yoshida must have begun putting poison into the water days ago. It was already affecting Mizuki when they met her at the fun run...

"How do you think it's worked, exactly?" Jessica asked, looking at the pipe.

"If that stuff is going into the water, it would have been impossible to avoid being poisoned. Every drink, every shower – and think about how the Academy is so proud of the hot springs there. The Japanese athletes have been soaking their bodies in poison every time they sit in those waters! But why on earth would Yoshida do this? What is he playing at?"

Josh rolled slightly to his left and craned his neck to look up at the rows of benches. *There you are, you fiend.* Right in the centre, near the back, Yoshida stood with his hands on his hips, watching the screen. About a dozen of his guards were there too, all in their matching black suits, sitting in silence. And there were two others, standing either side of Yoshida in white T-shirts and black tracksuit bottoms, their huge arms folded across their impossibly large chests...

Josh's mouth fell open, his chin smacking against the stone floor.

Chad and Brad Cooper!

"*What*?" Jessica mouthed. Then she rolled over and spotted the American wrestlers herself.

What were they doing here? What could they possibly be doing with Yoshida?

Suddenly up on the large screen flashed a picture of a room that must be at Edo Onsen, set up like a hospital ward, with doctors bustling between rows and rows of beds and men and women squirming on the sheets, pain and fever racking their bodies.

"Yoshida-san!"

The shout echoed through the huge cavern. Josh jumped, and beside him Jessica twitched – but it was the younger scientist, Doctor Harada, who had called out. He was leaning forwards on his chair.

"Please, Yoshida-san, do not continue with this. It is *mass murder*!"

"Shut up." Yoshida didn't shout – he snarled, like a wolf. A shiver ran down Josh's spine. "Do you think I wish this? You do not have to fear, when the Prime Minister pays my ransom, you will be permitted to deliver the antidote."

"The Prime Minister will never bow to your

demands," Doctor Maeda said, raising her head and staring up at Yoshida. "He has not returned your call, he will not!"

"I think he will," said Yoshida. "I am sure the lives of the Japanese athletes are worth ten billion yen. And they will die, within the hour, if the Prime Minister does not make the only sensible choice."

He's completely cracked, Josh thought. *This is the scheme of a total madman – a man who thinks he's untouchable.* "Within the hour," he breathed. "Jess…"

"I know." She looked at him, then back out towards the control panel. "We have to release the scientists, so they can stop the poisoning and can send the antidote – now!" His sister was right. There was no time to do anything else.

Josh pushed himself up onto his feet and sprinted into the middle of the amphitheatre, towards the three scientists. He heard a gasp of confusion from the horde of goons behind him, but he didn't look back; he pounded across the stone floor and with a hop and a skip he launched himself into a flying kick, taking down the guard who was standing over Professor Ito.

The guard crashed into the stone wall, hit his head and didn't get up again. Beside Josh, Jessica let out a cry of *"Hai!"* and performed a spinning back kick, leaning out of range of the middle guard's grabbing hands and chopping him in the neck with the side of her foot. He crumpled to the floor.

Jessica came out of the kick and landed in a crouch. The third guard balled his fists and charged at her. Josh leaped forward, planted his foot on her back and sprang into the air. He kicked out, *thwack thwack thwack*, planting three sharp blows in the guard's face before they both hit the ground – Josh on his feet, the guard on his back, unmoving.

Josh risked a look back at the amphitheatre. The dozen black-suited thugs were lining up on the edge of the flat space, standing still – waiting for their order.

"You," Yoshida growled. "I should have had you jailed when I had the chance. You two are even worse than Mimi. But I won't make that mistake again. Do you know where you are? This was the most secret of all samurai dojos. Ancient dynasties of warriors came here to prove their worth or die trying. To lose, in this

dojo, is to lose everything." He took in a deep breath.

You're enjoying this, Josh thought. *Linking yourself to the traditions of the past – but you're no samurai. I bet the odds weren't six to one back then, for a start.*

Yoshida threw out a hand, pointing to Josh and Jessica, and gave the order.

"Kill them."

Chapter Eleven

The men charged, like a herd of bulls in black suits. Josh flexed his shoulders, and then they were upon him in a tangle of punching fists and grabbing hands. Josh ducked out of the way of one punch, and another. He dropped to the ground and swept his legs in a circle, knocking at least one man to the ground, but his feet got caught and he had to roll away and get up.

Out of the corner of his eye he saw Jessica lay a hard punch on one thug's ear, sending him reeling.

Two victories weren't enough; there were two more guards behind that one and two more behind them...

Josh thrust out a mid-torso kick and heard a satisfying "Oof!" as it connected in the soft belly of one of Yoshida's goons. He lost his balance and stumbled back and felt huge arms, thick and stiff as steel girders, wrap around him and press him back against a hard chest. The goon behind him squeezed. Josh groaned as he felt his ribs creak and saw another brute charging right for him. He managed to bring his legs up right at the last second, planting his feet on the attacker's chest and pushing him away. His knees strained with the effort, but the goon stumbled back. The man who had him in a bear hug lost his footing and toppled, crying out as the hard stone floor winded him. His grip loosened and Josh moved with the momentum of their fall, somersaulting out of the man's arms and up to his feet.

Josh gasped in a couple of deep breaths. But there was no time for him to pause. Three more suited goons were closing in on him in a line, their arms out to stop him sprinting past them.

Always try to separate multiple attackers, Granny's voice echoed in his head.

Josh edged a little to the left, so the thug on that side reached him first and tried to punch him out instead of letting his friends catch up. Josh ducked the punch and grabbed the man's arm as it sailed past his head. When the middle goon drew his fist back Josh ducked behind the first thug, using him like a human shield. He felt the impact as the second man's punch landed squarely on the first one's chin.

"*Chikushō!*" the second goon swore as the shield's knees buckled. Josh shoved the unconscious man forwards, as hard as he could, and he fell on top of his colleague, taking him down.

One left from this little group... The last goon was standing and staring at Josh, clenching his fists furiously. Josh took one look at the man's wide stance and threw himself forward and down to slide between the man's legs.

As soon as he hit the stone floor he knew he'd made a mistake – it was unpolished and the friction grabbed him, stopping him halfway. He felt hands seize his ankles and he quickly twisted to stop his chin scraping along the ground as the goon dragged him back.

He caught a glimpse of Jessica backflipping across the floor with two lumbering thugs trying to grab her. Then the world seemed to lose all gravity, twisting upside down, and he flew through the air, swung by the ankles like an athlete's hammer...

THWACK.

Every bone in Josh's body seemed to rattle as he hit the stone wall. He slid to the floor, his feet still in the goon's grip.

It was the hardest sit-up he'd ever attempted, but although his head was spinning and his abdominal muscles screamed at him, Josh managed to reach up and grab the goon by the ears. The goon roared in pain and loosened his grip. Josh wrenched his feet free and drove them up into the man's gut.

Josh staggered to his feet, his whole body still shaking from the impact against the wall. There were three more thugs coming towards him. One had blood streaming from his nose and another had a black eye.

These guys just wouldn't lie down. *Well, that's*

something we've got in common.

Josh waited for them to come a little closer, then he vaulted up on the back of the goon he'd just kicked in the gut, who was still bent over and gasping in front of him. He took all his weight on one hand and swung his feet around in an arc, hitting each of the thugs in the face.

They stumbled, but they didn't fall down. Josh winced as he landed. Had he misjudged the distance or was he just getting tired?

"Argh!" Jessica groaned, somewhere to Josh's right. Josh just had time to see her go down under a pile of thugs when something hard and heavy hit him in the back and he smacked into the floor. Josh struggled and kicked out, and he felt his feet connect with something fleshy, but all he could see was the black suit jacket of the goon on top of him, and then there was a weight like a gorilla sitting on his chest...

Is this it? he wondered.

There was a *thud* somewhere above him and the goon pressed harder for a second. Then the pressure lifted. The man rolled away. Josh squirmed, punched and kicked his way out of the pile, and found the grey-haired scientist standing over him, holding one of the chairs like a club. He put out a hand and helped Josh up. Josh staggered to his feet, his head spinning for a moment.

"Jess..." he gasped. Professor Ito nodded to the other goon pile, where Doctor Harada was helping Jessica up while Doctor Maeda swung her chair hard into the face of a black-suited thug.

The goons kept trying to get up – but now the odds were in the twins' favour. Josh kicked out and knocked the one at his feet unconscious. He looked up in time to see Professor Ito bring his chair down on top of another one's head. The scientists weren't trained, but they were *angry*. It didn't take long for the five of them to lay out every one of Yoshida's dozen guards.

"Get the antidote ready," Jessica gasped, limping over to Professor Ito. The three scientists ran back to the control desk and Josh and Jessica turned to face Yoshida. Josh fought the urge to lean on Jessica's shoulder. He was pretty sure from the way she was standing that she would rather be leaning on him. But they stood apart and raised their chins in identical expressions of defiance.

Yoshida's eyes seemed more sunken than normal. His cheek was twitching.

"We won't let the athletes die," Jessica said. "We're going to stop you, Yoshida. No matter what it takes."

"This is not happening. This *will not happen*. You are just *children!*" Yoshida's eyes bugged and spittle flew from his lips.

We really got to him, Josh thought. *He's cracking up!*

"Boys!" Yoshida tapped the Cooper twins on their mountainous backs. They started to walk down the amphitheatre steps.

"Why would you two work for an evil man like Yoshida?" Josh shouted. "You're champions!"

"A million dollars, dude," one of the twins grunted.

"Like, *each*," the other one grinned.

"I'll cut you in for a full third of my profits if you stop those scientists releasing the antidote and then take these two out, permanently," Yoshida growled.

"Woah. A third. Uh, Brad," Chad turned to his brother. "Is that more than a million dollars?"

"Er..." Brad hesitated. "I dunno. Is it, Boss?"

"Yes," said Yoshida.

"Uh. Okay!" Chad and Brad nodded at each other.

"Okay, lil' dudes, stay still while we crush you," Brad rumbled.

The hospital ward flashed up on the screen again and this time Josh saw Mizuki in one of the hospital beds. She looked deathly pale. He pushed his anger to the back of his mind. *Focus.*

"How long do you need?" Josh asked Professor Ito.

"As long as you can give us," the professor answered.

Helpful, Josh thought, but he nodded and turned back to the advancing wrestlers.

"You take Chad, I'll take Brad," he said to Jessica.

"Fine. Okay. Which one's Chad?" she asked. Her voice was a little too light, too high. She was terrified.

Josh looked at the two hulking Americans striding across the floor towards them.

"I...don't know."

"Okay," Jessica said. "It's been nice knowing you, bro."

Chapter Twelve

Every instinct told Josh to run. In any other situation, running would be the right solution to the problem of being threatened by a pair of massive, ruthless champion wrestlers. Even the echo of Granny's teachings in his head was telling him to run.

But we can't, Josh thought. *If we let them get past us, they'll stop the antidote getting to Edo Onsen and all the athletes will die. What's your advice for a situation like that?*

Granny's voice stayed chillingly silent.

"Okay. Don't panic," said Jessica.

"Charge!" Josh cried. He ran at the Cooper twin on the left, probably Brad. Jessica sprang forwards, straight towards Chad.

Brad reached out, almost as if welcoming Josh into a hug. This wasn't going to work – Brad wouldn't need to avoid his blows, he'd just grab Josh in one of those brutal holds and it would all be over. The only thing Josh had left was the element of surprise. At the last minute he tumbled forwards into a handspring, flipping his legs up and smacking them into Brad's face.

He felt them connect, allowed himself a brief moment of triumph as he tucked and rolled away... but as he came up he could see that Brad had hardly even blinked. He was striding towards the scientists. Josh got in front of him and laid a few sharp punches on his chest, but Brad just swept a huge arm around and swatted him away, like an elephant using its trunk to swat a fly. Josh rolled as he hit the ground and got to his feet again in time to see Jessica launch a volley of spinning kicks at Chad, the flesh of his arms and shoulders rippling with each impact. The massive American didn't even break his stride. He pushed her aside as easily as if he was walking through a curtain.

Brad had reached the scientists.

"Hey," he grunted, grabbing Doctor Maeda by the back of her lab coat and dragging her away. "Leave it, lady."

Josh broke into a run, sprang into the air and aimed a high, flying kick at Brad's chest.

He felt a sickening twist in his ankle as his foot struck the man-mountain. He fell back, his foot throbbing. It was like kicking steel wrapped in concrete wrapped in thick rhino hide! But when he looked up he saw that Brad had dropped Doctor Maeda. As he reached for her, Josh aimed a kick at Brad's knee – it barely bent, let alone buckled, but Brad turned back to deal with Josh, which meant he was leaving the scientists alone.

Jessica saw her opportunity and got between Chad and Doctor Harada, who was laying a flurry of ineffectual but distracting punches and kicks on Chad's face and chest.

"Dude," Brad called out, "let's squash these twins first."

"Right, get the science dudes later," Chad agreed.

Mission accomplished...sort of, Josh thought, getting up and laying into Brad. He threw out uppercut punches and roundhouse kicks, somersaulting across the floor when Brad looked like he might grab him, gasping in breaths of air whenever he could, just trying to keep himself annoying but out of Brad's reach...

But Brad wasn't getting tired, and Josh could feel every movement getting harder now, his knees and elbows creaking and the skin on his knuckles and the bottoms of his feet getting hot and sore.

He knew the instant he'd thrown a punch that it wasn't quick enough. It felt like punching in slow motion through treacle, and he cringed as Brad's meaty hand closed around his wrist.

The wrestler's other hand came up and grabbed Josh's neck hard, and then in a flash of pink flesh, black-clad legs and a dull, screaming pain in Josh's elbow, Josh felt himself twisting over. He hit the floor on his back, a huge weight came down on his shoulder.

His arm was thrown out to one side. When the stars stopped dancing in front of his eyes, Josh realized he'd been caught in a flying arm-bar. He was lying on the floor with Brad's legs on top of him, either side of his arm, holding him down. If he tried to wriggle free, the Cooper twin would pull his arm off.

A guy this big should not *be able to do that!* Josh thought desperately.

He tried to bend his elbow, remembering everything he'd read about this position – it was all very well to say "lean into your opponent's legs" on paper, but when World Champion wrestler Brad Cooper was tugging on his arm like a ten-tonne weight, it was kind of hard to concentrate.

"Nyaah!" Jessica screamed. Josh's heart sank as he turned and saw her being pulled into a standing armlock, her knees buckling as Chad Cooper bent her arm right back.

Brad moved his legs, shoving one of his calves right up under Josh's throat. Josh choked, tried to suck in a last gasp of air, but the pressure was worse than four of Yoshida's goons. Blackness started to collect at the sides of his vision. He fought the urge to strain against Brad's grip – *don't pull, don't pull, if you do he'll break your arm...*

But if you don't pull back you'll choke...

Josh's throat burned and his chest felt like it would burst – and then he got an idea! He threw his head forward, almost crushing his own windpipe, and clamped his teeth down on Brad's leg.

"Aaaaauauuugh!" Brad howled, and his grip lifted. Josh gasped in a lungful of air and wriggled free, half staggering and half crawling away. He could taste blood, and when Brad sat up and looked at the back of his calf there was a neat row of red tooth-marks.

Not too honourable, Josh thought, *but it does the job.*

He seized one of the scientists' chairs and stumbled over to Chad, driving the leg of the chair towards his big shiny head. Chad ducked to avoid getting impaled, only just managing to get out of the way in time. He let go of Jessica and she somersaulted clear, holding her arm, as the chair hit the wall behind Chad and broke into pieces.

"Oh man," Brad said, getting to his feet. His voice was full of shock, as if Josh had just bitten him out of nowhere. "You little brat!"

"You bit my bro," Chad growled. "You're gonna *die*."

Josh rolled his arm around until he felt it click, and then squared up to Brad, with Jessica by his side, staring at Chad. The two sets of twins stood still for a second, looking at each other.

But what now? Josh swallowed hard. *They're still bigger and tougher than us...*

"Get 'em," Chad commanded, and the brothers started to march forward.

We need to bring them down to our size! Josh stepped forward and gave Jessica quick glance. She raised an eyebrow. Josh waved a hand quickly across from his ear to his nose. *Follow my lead*.

Brad Cooper lunged clumsily for him, but Josh dodged, rolled, and darted around behind them to pick up two of the broken chair legs. He tossed one through the air over Chad's head and Jessica caught it. Before Brad could turn around he ran up behind him and hacked at the back of his legs with the hard, splintered wood.

Josh ducked Brad's fists as he tried to swat him

away and kept on hacking at his legs, focusing his strikes as much as he could near the back of Brad's knees. Finally, with a grunt, Brad fell forwards until he was kneeling in front of Josh, his head now at striking height. Josh swung his chair leg like a baseball bat. He kept his glance focused on Brad's temple and made sure that the tip of the bat connected with that part of his opponent's skull. A direct hit! The American's eyes rolled back in his head and he dropped to the ground, out for the count.

"*Hai!*" Jessica cried. Chad had dropped to his knees as well. She brought her chair leg down on the top of his head and he joined his brother on the floor, unconscious.

Josh let out a breathless, near-hysterical burst of laughter. They'd won! Two kids from North London had beaten the world-famous Cooper twins! He ran over to Jessica and grabbed her into a hug, and only partly because he wasn't sure how much longer he could stand up.

"How did we pull that off?" Jessica gasped, gazing down at Chad and his brother, slumped on the floor.

Josh let his sister go. "They may be strong, but

their reactions were pretty slow. All that muscle bulk slowing them down."

Behind them, Doctor Maeda gave a supportive whoop as the three scientists worked to release the antidote, twisting dials and pressing buttons.

"How does the antidote work?" Jessica asked, darting over to the control board.

"By adsorption," Doctor Maeda explained. "We put other chemicals into the water and the poison is attracted. It clings to our chemicals and gets filtered out – if we're quick enough."

Clap, clap, clap.

Yoshida stood up, his hands slowly striking together – somehow, Josh didn't think you could call it applause.

"I see Mimi has trained you both well," Yoshida said. The rage had drained out of his face, but what was left behind was somehow worse. He was almost completely white, with dark, shrunken eyes. His face looked like a skull. "She has been getting in my way for more than fifty years, and until today, I have not truly held it against her. But I have had enough. I am more than an equal for any fighter. It's time for me to show my old fire."

He walked towards them, down the stone steps of the amphitheatre, peeling off the jacket of his suit.

A chilling burst of fear shuddered through Josh. His hands and feet ached like they might drop off, his arm felt stretched to breaking point, and he could hardly breathe. All he wanted to do was lie down on the cold stone floor and sleep for about a week.

Mr. Yoshida reached the bottom of the steps. He carefully unclipped his cufflinks and laid them on the stone bench.

"I am going to take great pleasure in breaking every bone in your bodies," he said, softly.

Jessica made a small noise in the back of her throat. Josh didn't have to look at her to know she was feeling pretty much as awful as him.

How were they going to stop Mr. Yoshida from snapping their necks like twigs?

Chapter Thirteen

Yoshida leaped through the air, his feet sweeping no more than a centimetre over Josh's head. He was as agile as any member of Team O.

Wherever Josh turned, Yoshida seemed to be there. It was as if he wasn't bound by the laws of space or gravity – he sprang across the room, grabbed hold of Josh's shirt and threw him down on his back on the hard stone floor. Josh dodged Yoshida's bony elbow as it sliced down towards his face. He leaped to his feet, but somehow Yoshida twisted so the same driving downwards movement turned into a spinning roundhouse kick. Yoshida's foot struck the side of Josh's head and blinding spots of light exploded in front of him.

Josh fell to the ground. He put his hand to his ear and it came away wet with blood.

He heard a *thump* and looked around, the whole cavern swimming. Jessica hit the stone floor shoulder-first and rolled crazily before landing in a crumpled heap.

Josh climbed to his feet, and ran at Yoshida. *No time for style. Have to take him down.*

He ducked Yoshida's punch and cannoned into him, grabbing for his tie. He let himself fall to the floor, the tie held tight in his hands, dragging Yoshida down with him. He heard a choking, gargling sound, and then a growl of fury. He tried to hold on, but his hands were slippery with sweat and blood, and Yoshida drew back his hand and slammed an open palm into Josh's chest.

It was like being thrown back by a bomb blast. Josh felt nothing but creaking agony in his chest as he flew, arms waving madly. And then something stabbed into his lower back and everything flashed to black. He heard himself yelling.

For a mad moment, Josh thought he must be dying. He must be impaled on something. He couldn't breathe.

But he was sitting up against something… Through a haze of pain and panic he let his head flop to the left and saw the edge of the control desk. He could move his shoulders, a little. He'd just hit the corner of the metal desk. He wasn't impaled. He was alive.

He couldn't move, though. He tried to control his breathing and stand up but his feet wouldn't do what he told them.

Fuzzily, he heard Yoshida's voice. "Out of the way!" He looked up. Yoshida had thrown Professor Ito aside and was stabbing at the controls. "Time's up. The Prime Minister has not responded. He is responsible for this."

"What are you doing?" Doctor Harada demanded. Yoshida slapped him aside, without turning from the controls.

"Dumping the antidote into Tokyo Bay. There will be no cure."

"No!" Doctor Maeda cried. "There's no way we'll be able to make another batch in time – they'll die! They'll all die!"

"Indeed," said Yoshida. "And all of Japan will know I am not a man to be trifled with."

Josh struggled to his knees. He felt like someone had tied weights to every one of his muscles. He told his legs to move but nothing happened. *Is it all over? Have we failed?*

Then a furious shape flew through the air, out of the black patch on Josh's peripheral vision, and hit Yoshida's back. It clung on, one arm around his neck, legs around his waist.

Jessica!

Yoshida staggered backwards under her weight. As the scientists leaped to the controls, furiously trying to undo what he'd done, Yoshida twisted and turned, seizing handfuls of Jessica's hair.

Get him, Jess…don't let go…

Yoshida let out a roar and gripped Jessica's wrist in his clawed fingers. He threw her off and she slammed into the wall, as light and limp as a rag doll. She fell to the floor, and didn't move.

No!

Josh rose to his feet, washed up on a wave of anger.

"That's my sister," he said. His tongue felt huge in his mouth.

"It *was* your sister," Yoshida smirked.

Josh staggered forwards, throwing his whole weight behind a clumsy punch that Yoshida caught in one hand. Josh tried to sweep Yoshida's feet out from under him, but he was so weak Yoshida didn't even bother to move, and the impact did nothing.

Josh saw the back of Yoshida's hand coming towards him as if in slow motion, and couldn't move to duck. It hit him across the face and sent him spinning through the air. The floor passed by his face three times before he smacked into it.

He looked up. Yoshida was walking to the controls. The scientists cringed back...

"Not beaten yet," Josh slurred.

Yoshida stopped. He turned around.

Josh got to his feet. He sort of didn't know how – his legs felt like bad bamboo, his arms like wet noodles. He knew he was shaking all over. He blinked away the tears of pain that streamed down his face, and it nearly made him so dizzy he fell down again.

"I'm not beaten," he muttered. "Don't you want to win?"

Yoshida took a step towards him. Then another.

"C'mon," Josh said. He was swaying madly, or maybe that was just the cavern rolling and tipping under his feet. "Want to beat the Muratas? Have to… keep me down first."

Yoshida marched towards him, breaking into a run at the last minute and laying a punch on Josh's neck that felt like it might push right through and make his head fall off. Josh grabbed Yoshida's shirt and stayed on his feet. He couldn't find the energy for a blow so he simply clung on. Yoshida's knee slammed into Josh's stomach and he doubled over, his hands slipping off the shirt, and the ground came up to meet him like an old friend.

He tried to say *no*, but it came out as "Nnn," as he pushed himself to his knees. Yoshida lashed out with a low back kick that slammed into Josh's chest.

Get up.

No… The stalactites on the ceiling circled like

birds, calling out to him. *Stay down. It's no use. He's going to kill you.*

But there's no other hope for the people he's murdering. The thought got him up again. He planted his feet on the hard stone. He couldn't even stand up straight – his back twitched and spasmed when he tried – but he was up.

"Oy," he managed.

He couldn't see Yoshida. He only heard him howl. "Why won't you *just stay down*!?"

"Because he's a Murata," said a voice.

Granny!

Josh raised his head. A crowd of black-clad figures stood in the entrance to the cavern – a group of lithe, hooded people flanked by what looked like hundreds of bulky, armoured men wearing helmets and holding massive rifles.

Josh sank to his knees as Team O rushed into the room. Every part of his body hurt – and at the same time, he felt like he couldn't feel anything at all. The figure he thought was Granny grabbed Yoshida, expertly dodging his blows.

"Give it up, Noboru," she growled.

The tallest ninja – Mimasu? – struck out at Yoshida and when he ducked away a thin, black-clad shape raised two pairs of nunchakus, spinning them a centimetre from the Yakuza's nose. Mr. Yamamoto!

Yoshida tried to duck and roll away but another ninja blocked his path.

Team O had him surrounded. One of the policemen stepped forwards, not quite into Yoshida's reach, and passed Granny a set of handcuffs.

"Yoshida Noboru, you are under arrest..."

The control panel beeped, and there was a hissing sound from the antidote tanks.

"This is Doctor Maeda..." The world was getting blurry, but Josh could make out the scientist holding a police radio to her ear. "Get the patients to the hot springs, the antidote is being pumped in there now. Hurry!"

"This isn't over, Mimi," Yoshida's voice screamed through the fog. "You haven't seen the last of me!"

He really has seen too many Bond movies, Josh thought, and he blacked out.

* * *

Josh leaned forward in his swivelling leather chair, his eyes fixed on the big screen in Team O's secret underground base. The screen showed a huge crowd of cheering people waving flags and banners, lining a wide empty street. Jessica twisted her fingers in the hem of her T-shirt and Kiki poured another serving of tea into Mr. Yamamoto's cup.

Josh sighed as he looked around the base. Even though it hurt to move, it felt great to be back, just like coming home – especially since Granny had entrusted him and Jessica with the code for the secret lift, so they could get in by themselves. He didn't know anyone else with access to a secret ninja lair with surveillance equipment that covered the whole of Tokyo, plus a wall full of traditional samurai weaponry.

Kiki was looking around the base too, still taking it all in with wide eyes. She poured a cup of tea for Granny with a little seated bow. "Thank you, *Obaa-sama*, for inviting me to share this event with you here – I am so honoured to be trusted like this."

"It is the least we could do to thank you for helping Josh and Jessica while we were indisposed," said Granny.

"How did you get out of prison, by the way?" Kiki asked.

"Yoshida helped us out," said Sachiko, grinning with her mouthful of sparkling false teeth.

"*What*?" Josh and Jessica chorused.

"The government agency we work for would have stepped in to vouch for us eventually," Granny said, "even though Yoshida went to some lengths to convince the police not to believe we were on their side."

"But as soon as Yoshida called the Prime Minister to make his demands, the Minister tried to call us," said Sachiko, "and that was how he discovered we were imprisoned. He had us released right away!"

"So, Yoshida caused his own downfall!" Kiki laughed.

"As usual," said Granny dryly. "He really made a mistake in threatening the athletes. He will go to prison for a very, ver long time."

"Shh, all of you. Here she comes!" said Nana. On the screen a group of runners turned the corner onto the street, and the camera angle adjusted to take in a large white arch with a red ribbon across it. Josh spotted Mizuki the Marathon Princess, in her distinctive purple running gear, just as she put on a burst of speed.

"C'mon, Mizuki, you can do it..." Jessica gasped. The crowd went wild as Mizuki passed them and a few seconds later she burst through the ribbon and slowed to a jog, her arms raised in victory. The camera zoomed in. She was sweating, but glowing with health. A spinning graphic of a gold medal appeared in the bottom corner of the screen.

"And that's it," said the commentator, "Mizuki, Tokyo's Marathon Princess, has taken the gold medal for Japan, after the Japanese athletics team's miraculous recovery from the illness that nearly devastated the host nation's chances..."

Mr. Yamamoto turned and winked at Josh. Josh grinned back. Nobody would ever know the Japanese athletes almost didn't make it to the World Championships at all!

"Nana-san, are you reading me?" Mr. Nakamura's voice rang out from the speakers beside the TV screen.

"Good timing, Nakamura-san," said Nana, pulling

her chair up to the control desk. "Mizuki just won gold!" She swiped a few buttons and the picture on the monitor switched to a CCTV view of a Tokyo street. Josh tried to spot Mr. Nakamura. He knew that the elderly medical expert had had to miss watching the marathon because he was out on a mission, but he couldn't see him.

"He's out of the shop and I'm giving chase," said Mr. Nakamura, as on the screen a figure leaped forward, chasing after a man all in black who had just come barrelling out of a jewellery shop. The figure giving chase was a woman, in a traditional Japanese kimono…or was it? Josh looked at Sachiko, the team's disguises expert, who gave him a twinkly smile.

On the screen, Mr. Nakamura, still in the kimono, kicked off his wooden sandals and sped up, moving faster than an 87-year-old really ought to be able to. He took a flying leap and brought the young man down with a kick to the back of the neck.

"Good work, Nakamura-san," said Granny.

"Do Team O ever take a day off?" Jessica asked.

"We do not," said Granny. "We had plenty of time off in jail," she added, with a smile.

On the screen, uniformed police were swarming around the jewel thief, and Mr. Nakamura handed him over to them and then slipped away. As he walked off, his microphone caught one of the policemen speaking to the other: "Who was that old lady?"

Nana laughed, and Sachiko took a bow.

"Speaking of disguises," Granny said, rising from her chair, "I have something for you two." She went over to one of the gleaming metal lockers and opened it to reveal two neat piles of black cloth.

"Is that..."

"Can we..."

Josh and Jessica reached out to receive their brand-new ninja outfits.

"You two really proved yourselves this week," Granny said. "I feel that, considering your performance – and considering that your parents have agreed that you should stay in Tokyo a little longer – there is no reason why you should not take part in missions as fully-fledged members of Team Obaasan. In which case, you'll need something to wear."

Josh and Jessica exchanged a high five, and Josh pulled on the ninja hood, feeling the lightness of the material and the way the built-in camera and microphone sat against his skin.

"But will there be much for us to do," Jessica asked, "with Yoshida behind bars?"

Granny smiled, her skin wrinkling around her eyes. "Team O is always on call. Crime never ends, and we'll be ready for it. I'm sure we'll need your help. If you're ready?"

Josh grinned, and together the twins bowed to their ninja grandmother. "Ready, willing, able – and with the uniform to prove it!"

Don't miss more high-kicking ninja action from Josh and Jess in...

Out now

Out now